Millennium Knight

JLee

outskirtspress
DENVER, COLORADO

This is a work of fiction. The events and characters described herein are imaginary and are not intended to refer to specific places or living persons. The opinions expressed in this manuscript are solely the opinions of the author and do not represent the opinions or thoughts of the publisher. The author has represented and warranted full ownership and/or legal right to publish all the materials in this book.

Millennium Knight
All Rights Reserved.
Copyright © 2012 Janet Lee
v8.0

Cover Illustration © 2012 Janet Lee.

This book may not be reproduced, transmitted, or stored in whole or in part by any means, including graphic, electronic, or mechanical without the express written consent of the publisher except in the case of brief quotations embodied in critical articles and reviews.

Outskirts Press, Inc.
http://www.outskirtspress.com

ISBN: 978-1-4327-7865-1

Library of Congress Control Number: 2011915973

Outskirts Press and the "OP" logo are trademarks belonging to Outskirts Press, Inc.

PRINTED IN THE UNITED STATES OF AMERICA

MILLENNIUM KNIGHT

JLee

Dedicated to:
My sons Jordan and Dylan,
who are my true inspiration.

My husband Bill for his support,
My Mum Joyce who encouraged me,
My sister Sue Johnstone for sharing her
extensive knowledge of digital techniques.
Thanks.

Cover design & interior illustrations:
JLee

Calder's Glossary

Aye=Yes
Heigh-ho=Hello
Hey Up (Yorkshire greeting)=Hello
Good morrow=Good day
Fare thee well=Farewell, goodbye
Mark my word=Believe me
Thee, thou=You
Thy, Thine=Your, yours

Hast or hath=Has or have
Keepeth=Keep, keeps
Knoweth=Know, knows
Giveth=Give, gives

Methinks=I think
Hither and thither=Here and there
Whither?=Where?
Kirk=Church
Verily=Truly
Post haste=Right away
Ginnel=Narrow passageway

Goodfellow=Friend
Clodhopper=Clumsy person
Clumperton=Fool
Knave=Dishonest person
Doppelganger=Double, or spirit twin
Troll=An elf-like creature
Thievery=Stealing, theft
Jorvik=Viking name for the City of York
Modus Travelendi=Mode of travel

Nay=No
Prithee=Please

Laiking=Playing
Thou art=You are
Outta=Out of

Wilt=Will
Wouldst=Would
Doth=Does
Mayest=Might, may

Leastwhile=At least

Wert=Were
Beck=Stream
Over Yonder=Over there
Anon=Later
Afore=Before

Scarpered=Ran away

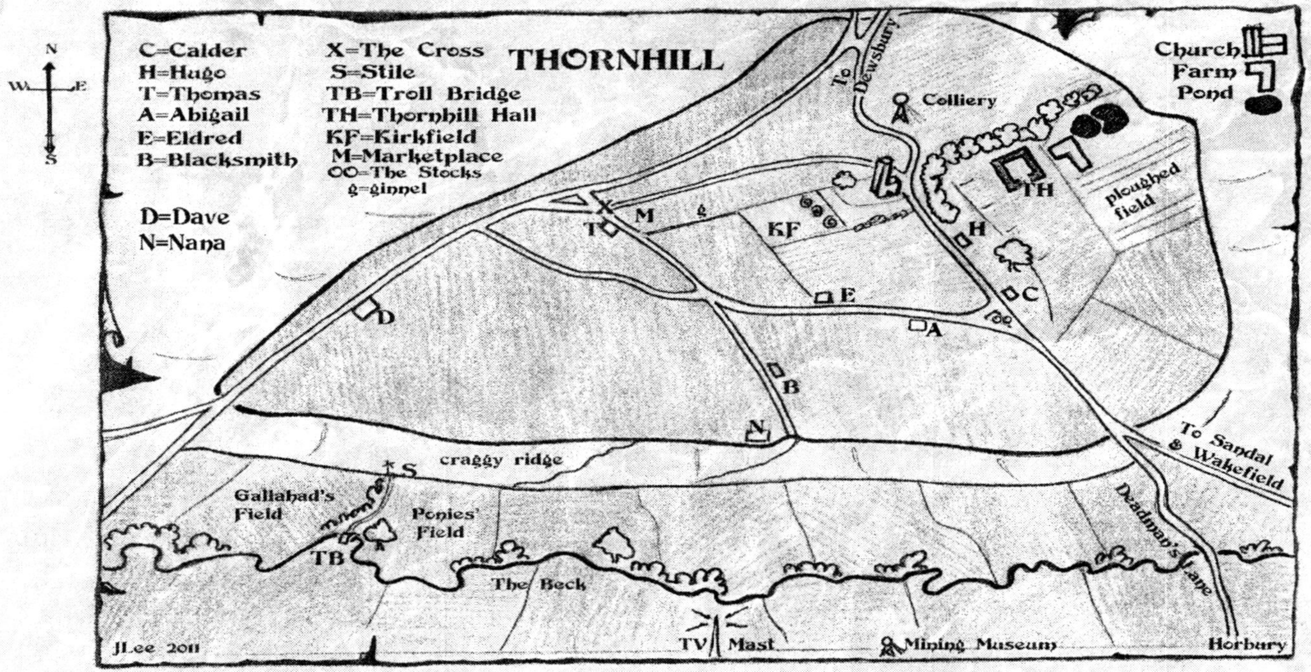
THORNHILL
C=Calder
H=Hugo
T=Thomas
A=Abigail
E=Eldred
B=Blacksmith
D=Dave
N=Nana
X=The Cross
S=Stile
TB=Troll Bridge
TH=Thornhill Hall
KF=Kirkfield
M=Marketplace
OO=The Stocks
g=ginnel
N
W
E
S
To Dewsbury
Colliery
Church
Farm
Pond
ploughed field
To Sandal & Wakefield
Deadman's Lane
craggy ridge
Gallahad's Field
Ponies' Field
The Beck
TV Mast
Mining Museum
Horbury
JLee 2011

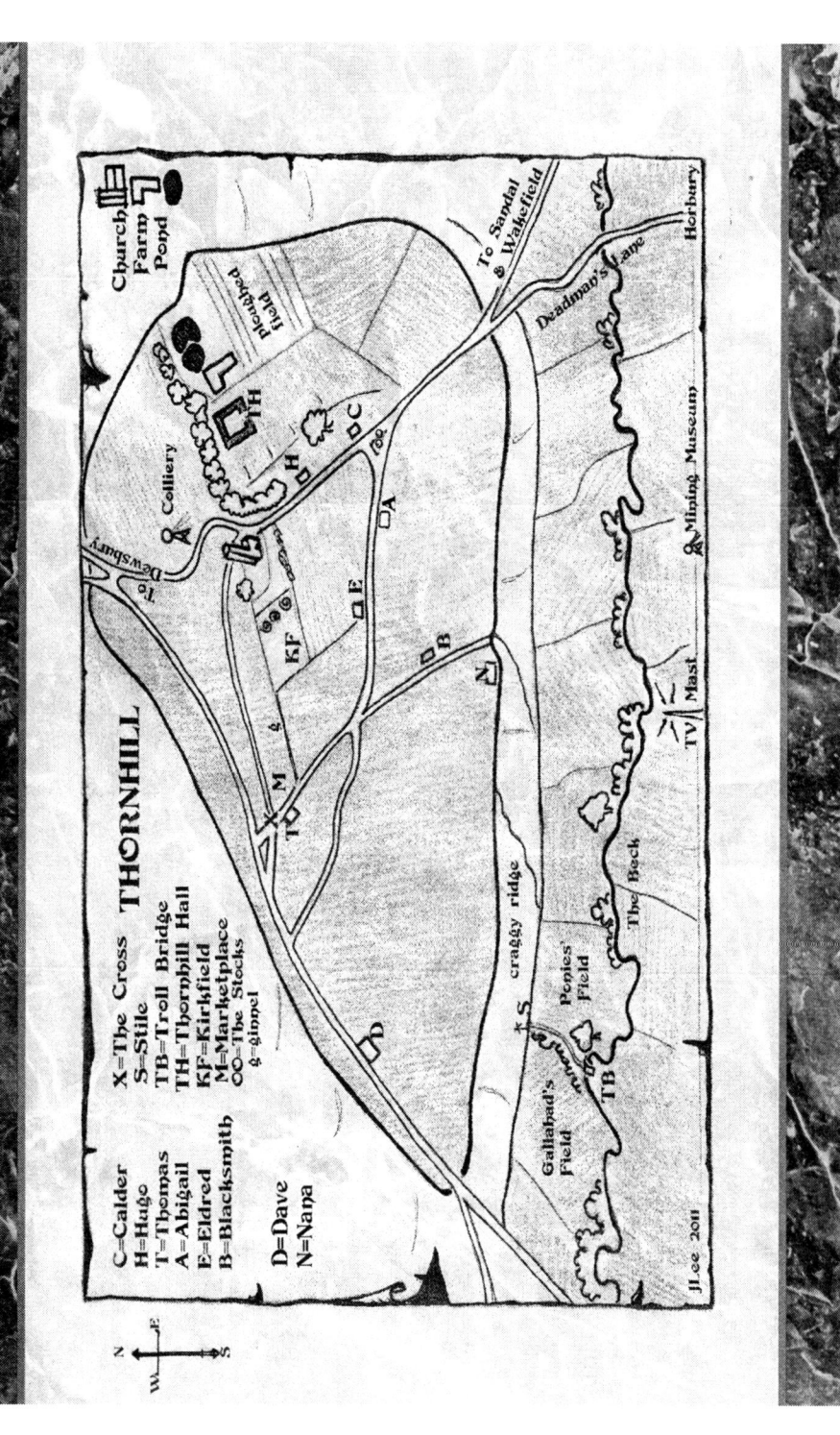

Outta Sight

Calder landed on his bottom, on the stone wall in his own back yard. His heart pounded and his mind buzzed excitedly.

"FAN-bloomin'-TASTIC!" he exhaled, staring up at the azure California sky. Moments earlier he had been thundering through a royal jousting tournament in medieval England, perched precariously on the back of a chestnut mare, his lance aimed at the gleaming chest-plate of his opponent, Sir Jordan de Thornhill.

"Wow! Medieval England was a blast!! That was no daydream -- time-travel is definitely for real," he concluded wildly, checking to make sure he'd sustained no injury from his return journey.

He might have looked like any other eleven-year-old boy, sitting aimlessly on his backyard wall, staring off into space, but inside Calder's tousled head numerous possibilities of time and space continued to unfold as he waited for his cue to perform. Instead of a line from past to present, Calder visualized clusters of moments, like a mass of bubbles, with only a thin membrane separating one era from the next.

He reflected for a moment as he caught his breath. Maybe I slipped through the wall between two adjacent moments. Time-travel might not reach back or forward, it might just press through sideways, he postulated. He liked the idea of making a lateral move to his favorite era, the Middle Ages. In fact, he'd thought of himself as a displaced knight ever since his last visit to England.

Meanwhile, inside Calder's house, another strange reality was being played out.

"What are we supposed to see?" squeaked one voice.

"It's so-o-o dark in here," sighed a second.

"I can't even see my hands!" balked another.

"Ouch, somebody stepped on my toes."

"I see nothing, n-o-t-h-i-n-g!"

"Relax and let your eyes adjust to the dark, then you'll see," answered Jenna. Hers was the only adult voice inside the darkened cube.

"I feel as though we're waiting for magic to happen," whispered Azule.

"Or like a ghost is about to materialize before our very eyes," added Joe. Both were correct in a more scientific sort of way.

"Are you all facing this way?" Jenna asked, tapping her fingers on the plastic curtain that formed the cube. There was a shuffling of feet, then a unanimous "Yeah," as Jenna removed the tiny square of masking tape, and a pinhole of light shone through at eye level.

"Imagine being inside a camera and this pinhole is

the lens letting in the light," Jenna began, but before anyone had time to turn their heads, Calder shattered the moment by rustling the plastic and moaning, "Oooo--ooo--ooh!"

The students inside let out a blood-curdling shriek, scared out of their wits after anticipating ghosts.

"No, really, listen. This is too crazy," railed Calder. "I was in a jousting tournament in medieval England -- fell off my horse, and landed -- Whoomph! -- on the backyard wall! A time warp or something!"

Jenna opened a slit in the plastic and peered out. "Another time-warp, Calder? Could you please try to stay with us -- I mean, in the present -- at least for the duration of the class?" Jenna was Calder's mom and she was used to his vivid imagination. "Anyway," she continued, "we need you to entertain us on the wall outside, to illustrate how this camera works." Her dining room had been transformed into a huge walk-in camera for her summer photography class; it became a *camera obscura* in effect.

"Okay, lights, camera, action!" Jenna yelled after Calder had returned to the wall. It was the cue he had been waiting for earlier. Slightly disheartened by their lack of interest in his medieval meanderings, Calder shrugged his shoulders, but then sprang into action.

Inside the cube, the ray of light flickered like a miniature movie theater.

"Look at Calder. He's upside down!" gushed Sarah, focusing on the inverted image.

"He's waving his hands and stomping his feet," added Azule.

"Now he's doing jumping-jacks," continued Derick.

"How can we see him when he's really outside?" Joe chimed in.

"And where's the projector?" asked Adam.

"I'll explain in a moment," Jenna promised, slipping a prism in front of the pinhole. In an instant everything changed; shafts of light splintered into vibrant little rainbows all around the darkened room.

"WOW!" they gasped, "WAY COOL!" They enjoyed the prismic effects for several minutes before taking down the black plastic. Daylight spilled in from all sides, and once again the cube became Jenna's dining room.

"Okay, form a circle with your chairs," shouted Jenna, tossing the plastic into the garage for recycling. As she entered the back room, she was surprised to find her students sitting in place, but laughing hysterically. Through the windows, Calder could be seen prancing around on the wall, still making ape faces and scratching furiously at his armpits like a comical gorilla. Derick, Joe, and Adam were encouraging him to continue his zany antics, but Calder finished with a bow, then leaped from the wall, and ran in through the open door.

"Thank you for your outstanding Shakespearian performance," Jenna laughed.

"Ah! Friends, Romans, countrymen, lend me your ears..." Calder uttered, as he grabbed for Derick's ears. Then he slid into base on the shag rug, slashing the air with his imaginary sword. He couldn't resist just one more dramatic moment, but invariably he stretched it too far.

"Sit down, Goofball!" laughed Derick.

"He's so annoying," whispered Sarah impatiently.

The teacher counted backwards. "Three -- two -- one." Calder sprang up and sat tall in the only available chair, exaggerating his attentiveness, so Jenna resumed the lesson.

"Would anyone care to comment on the moving image inside our camera?"

"We could see Calder pirouetting on the wall outside," answered Sarah.

"Why was he upside down, and where was the projector?" asked Jenna, repeating their own questions from earlier.

After a few misguided answers, Calder offered his suggestion. "It's an inverted image, and there is no projector -- only the magic of the light!" He added an intriguing observation. "Have you ever noticed how, on the convex side of a spoon you're right side up, but on the concave side you're inverted?"

"Yes, exactly!" Jenna exclaimed, glad to see that he'd settled down again. Calder had participated in many of her art and science lessons, and he also had a few of his own theories. Jenna continued to explain how an image automatically turns itself upside-down as light passes through a pinhole. Not magic, but a natural phenomenon.

"Our eyes work in the same way. Light inverts as it passes through the pupil, and the inverted image lands on the retina at the back of the eye."

"So why don't we see everything upside down as it would be on the retina?" queried Derick. Jenna continued with her long explanations of how the brain makes sense of the image by turning it back the right way.

"Okay, okay, cut! I'm just not feeling it here," Calder interjected rudely in a high-pitched, affected voice, which started the whole class giggling. He had a repertoire of character voices. His impersonation of a fervent Movie Director was hilarious. "What I want to see are swashbuckling alligators and pirates bursting onto the scene -- not a lecture!" he lisped with great drama.

Jenna flashed Calder a look of exasperation, but then decided to allow the disruption; it was summer and she welcomed the hearty laughter of the group.

"Bring that kind of creative thinking into your photography, and I promise we can use your swashbuckling alligators, your pirates, and your jousting knights, in our film-making class. Okay, grab your cameras and let's go and focus on whatever subjects you like in the backyard," directed Jenna. "Remember to look for unusual angles, close-ups, patterns..." her voice trailed off.

Azule paused on the way out to look at the artwork on the walls. Calder's drawing, *Self-Portrait in Blue,* was proudly displayed among some other still-life compositions. His eyes were closed and he was laughing. His shoulders formed a rainbow above a mouse and a hawk, and behind his head the background split: light blue sky above multi-colored meadows on the left, and dark blue sky with a distant castle on the right.

"Calder looks happy with his pets, but he appears to be in two worlds at one time!" she remarked.

How true! thought Jenna, complimenting Azule on her acute observations. Then like a bag of spilled jaw-breakers, the students bounced off in all directions to photograph the back garden.

Calder grabbed Derick and Joe by the elbows. "While I was waiting on the wall a weird thing happened, like a time warp or something!" he gestured excitedly. "It happened once before when I was in England, only this time, I was charging full speed ahead in a jousting tournament. My helmet and visor were way too big. Sweat was pouring down my face, stinging my eyes. I raised my lance, trying to keep my balance. Then I focused on the chest plate of my fast-approaching foe, Sir Jordan. He's a gnarly brute, twice my size!" -- Calder paused to see his friends' reactions before continuing. "I hit his chest plate square on, but the impact, Man! It sent shock waves all up my arm, almost dislocated my shoulder, and sent me flying into a backward flip over the rump of my galloping charger. All I remember was hitting the ground with a THUD! Then I realized I'd somehow landed, smack -- back on the wall in this millennium! Right over there. It was AWESOME! -- Well, except for the pain!"

Derick and Joe laughed. "Time warp? Charger? Jousting tournament?" They figured Calder had gone off into one of his wild imaginings again, so they headed off towards the deck, laughing and shaking their heads.

Jenna slipped quietly back into the kitchen and threw a bag of three-minute popcorn into the microwave. She opened a bottle of apple juice and poured it into six paper cups, positioning them around the dining table with a bowl of grapes at their center, then she went out to see if anyone needed help.

Her students were all busy experimenting with their cameras, figuring out focus, and trying to create unusual compositions. Jenna gave them a few more minutes -- then called, "Snack time!" They didn't need to be asked twice.

"I enjoyed looking through the prism you showed us today," offered Adam, stuffing his mouth with popcorn.

"Yeah, the light split into all the colors of a rainbow," added Sarah. "Like dancing spectrums in a black cube!"

"I wonder if the plural of spectrum would be spectra?" pondered Azule dreamily.

"I liked the fish-eye lens," said Joe. "I could see my feet and the ceiling at the same time."

"Yeah, it turned the whole backyard into a time-warp bubble," observed Calder, thinking back to his amazing medieval experience.

On Tuesday, the students arrived to find a tall tripod in the living room, with Jenna's digital camera fastened firmly on top. It was aimed towards a large ceramic vase on the coffee table, and was lit by a bright lamp on the right side, creating a high contrast image. Jenna immediately dispersed the kids in search of interesting objects for their own still-lifes. Calder chose to photograph his Norman helmet, which he had bought in a museum gift shop in Whitby, England, sixty miles from where his nana lived. He had used all his vacation allowance on that one item; it was his pride and joy!

Calder carefully arranged the shiny steel helmet on top of a crumpled red velvet curtain, otherwise known as his medieval cloak.

"Look carefully at the reflections," cautioned Jenna. "Try to avoid showing the camera, the light, or yourself in the helmet." Taking her advice, Calder moved the spotlight a little farther towards the rear, lighting the background. He had become very serious now that his helmet was being featured. He aimed the camera at the dull nose guard and focused. The helmet still showed enough cool reflections in the shiny hand-beaten steel. It contrasted well against the softly lit folds of the deep sanguine velvet cloak and the ripple of cascading chain mail.

Calder gazed deeply into the reflections and noticed a speck that seemed to hover high above a green pasture.

He was puzzled; there was nothing so green around the room. Staring further, he saw that the hovering speck was a golden hawk. But how could that be? As he concentrated on the impressive hawk, it plunged low into the countryside and Calder's mind followed, forgetting the still-life and the photography class. He was once again in the ancient village of Thornhill, kicking up crisp dry leaves as he followed the swirling stream, which meandered along its ancient course in the valley below his nana's house.

The hawk re-emerged clutching a stunned rodent in its talons and flew up to a high branch. Calder held his breath, not wanting to disturb the awesome sight in front of him. He studied the soft speckled plumage, the powerful talons, and the hawk's razor-sharp beak as it tore into its pitiful prey. He felt sorry for the forlorn rat, but intrigued by such a wild display of nature.

Regaining his composure, Calder focused on the babbling stream as it gently splashed over boulders, and ultimately disappeared under an ancient footbridge in the tangled ferns below. He felt calm and in tune with his surroundings. The evening sun was dipping into the western horizon, casting long vibrant rays onto the oak branch, and illuminating the magnificent auburn hawk with a golden glow.

"Are you going to photograph it or just admire it?" quipped Sarah in a sarcastic tone of voice. Derick and Adam snickered too. They had all been observing Calder for several minutes, sitting motionless with his gaze glued to the helmet, his eyes vacant and glazed over as if he were in a faraway dream.

"Oh, yeah, huh!" gasped Calder, snapping out of his trance. He checked the focus in the L.C.D. screen, then proceeded to capture a perfect shot, silently hoping the heraldic scene would be frozen forever in the reflections of his helmet.

That night Calder took his Norman helmet and carefully replaced it on the wooden stand in his bedroom, gazing deeply in search of his vision. He wondered if he had side-stepped into one of the time bubbles he'd pondered earlier. I *am* a time-traveler! Calder reassured himself, polishing the helmet with his tee-shirt sleeve. It certainly is not my imagination. Adults were forever reassuring him that he, "Merely had a vivid imagination," but he knew better than to rely on their misconceptions of reality.

He slid under the covers, keeping his eyes focused on the highly polished metal. He had recognized the bridge. Yes, he was sure of it. It was there, in that exact meadow, that Calder had experienced his first strange time-warp, one that still perplexed him. Why twice in the same place? Could it possibly be that these were just daydreams? He thought for a moment -- No! That was out of the question, they were too REAL. But had he actually slipped into a parallel existence? Had he traveled back or sideways in time? Calder vowed to figure out how to take control of this phenomenon, so he could return to the pastoral scene at will.

Wednesday's photo theme was *Fashion*. Azule spilled the contents of Jenna's two vintage suitcases onto the floor.

"I'm wearing this outfit!" announced Sarah, grabbing a circular skirt before anyone else had a chance. She pulled her hair back into a ponytail and donned a pair of rhinestone sunglasses. "I'm going for the fifties look," she added, tightening a wide belt snugly around her waist, and finishing it off with a pair of gold stiletto-heeled shoes. Calder manned the lighting, Joe checked the pose, and Derick crooned sarcastically, "Diamonds are a girl's best friend." Sarah laughed, tilting her head back ever so slightly, then Joe froze the moment in a Hollywood flash.

"Nice *Monroe* shot, Dude!" laughed Calder. He had temporarily dismissed his vision of the hawk at Thornhill as a momentary lapse of concentration. Yes, a mere daydream. He was once again enjoying being a young photographer. Well, for now anyway!

Adam had brought along a wonderful prop: his dry ice/smoke machine.

"Let's use that for atmosphere on Azule's photo," suggested Derick eagerly.

Over her shorts and tank-top, Azule chose to wear a Victorian petticoat and a silk blouse. Sitting cross-legged in front of the swirling backdrop, she positioned the 1960's Gibson across her lap and pretended to strum. She wore a beaded headband, and let her black hair cascade down to her waist, like a somber young folk-singer, promoting peace. Adam flicked on the smoke machine as the mist crept around Azule's feet and rose thinly to her knees, making her appear to hover above a wispy floating fog. Joe checked the lighting, and this time Derick captured the soulful shot.

Finally the boys had their turn to pose as the girls took over the camera production. Everyone headed outside to set up in front of the garage, where Jenna's painting of a gigantic ocean wave served as a backdrop. Balancing precariously on the surfboard, Joe struck a cool *hang-ten* surfer pose. As his toes edged the nose of the board, he arched his back and yelled, "Surf's Up!" Sarah seized the moment and snapped the shot.

After Joe's cool shot, Calder threw himself onto the board in a dramatic *wipeout* pose. With the board careening to the right and his feet sticking up behind him, he looked as though he'd been spit savagely, cannonball-style, from inside the painted wave. Azule was ecstatic. "Totally tubular, Calder!" she declared, looking into the L.C.D. screen at her convincing results.

After a week of experimental photography and fun, Friday arrived, and by noon the back room had been transformed into a veritable picture gallery, a collective exhibition displayed for all the parents to see. Joe's *Monroe* shot was a classic, Derick's photo of Azule in the fog was lyrically dreamy, and there were some exceptional outdoor perspectives too. Calder's high contrast photo of the Norman helmet had turned out extremely well, but he was slightly disappointed that the hawk in the meadow wasn't visible.

The six young photographers were now ready for their *Grand Finale*. Having devoured a large pizza, their sundaes arrived in all their glory -- six colorfully cloned, fruit n' cream mountains.

"This sundae rocks!" declared Adam, as Sarah rolled her eyes in ecstasy and popped another crimson cherry into her mouth.

At 2:45, their parents arrived, bustling and chatting as they made their way up the driveway and into the makeshift gallery. Every student was proudly showing off their creative accomplishments. Utterances of *Wow!* and *Awesome!* were heard over and over. Finally, someone managed a couple of full sentences: "These compositions are truly extraordinary, Jenna! What subject are you teaching next summer?"

"Next year, Film-making and Animation Techniques!" Jenna answered.

"Sign us up!" yelled Derick and Joe in unison.

"Yeah, move over Nick Parks," laughed Adam.

Calder had other things on his mind. With his eyes fixed on his helmet, he was calculating the possibility that time was much more flexible than a straight line from past -- to present -- and on into the future. It seemed far more convoluted than that!

Overlapping realities? Wormholes? Parallel universes? Moebius strips? He must find out -- and the sooner the better!

Yin and Yang

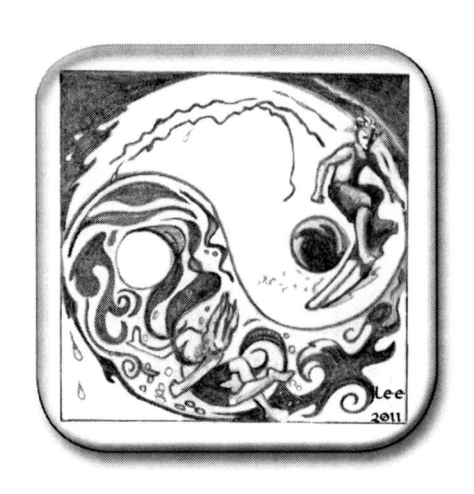

There was a buzz circulating the school playground; chatter and excitement exuded the usually nonchalant pre-teens. Tonight was their sixth-grade dance and kids from all north county schools were invited.

"My Mom says she'll take us to the mall before the dance," announced Sarah. "Do y' wanna come with us, Azule?"

"I'd love to," answered Azule, "but I'll have to ask my mom first."

"Jade's coming too," continued Sarah. "Bring a few dollars to spend."

"Okay, I'll be at the flagpole if I can go," replied Azule.

As the boys nudged the girls through the double doors, the bell rang and the buzz was momentarily quelled.

"Boys are so immature!" declared Sarah with an air of feigned disgust, while another group of girls giggled their way back into the classroom and settled at their desks.

Azule pulled out her social sciences book as Calder entered the room, singing: *"Talkin' 'bout my g-g-generation."* He was usually in high spirits, that is, when he wasn't daydreaming or being heckled by one of his adversaries. His desk was at the opposite end of the classroom from Azule. They had always been friends, but by sixth grade an invisible barrier seemed to exist between some boys and girls. Calder smiled awkwardly in her direction.

"Scruffy hairball!" snarled Cody Kenyon derisively as he nudged Calder's desk. Calder had been tormented by this devious character for a long time, dodging his disparaging remarks, and shrugging away from his snarling glances. They had once been friends, but things had turned sour in third grade. Cody had never been able to appreciate Calder's individuality or his creative, questing spirit, and had forever been trying to control or bully him.

In fifth grade it had almost come to blows when Cody had circulated some malicious rumors about Calder. Feeling humiliated, Calder had threatened to punch him on the nose after school. After years of being heckled, Calder had finally retaliated. However, neither slander, nor threats were taken lightly and both boys had been given detentions. The Principal had made sure they were in different home rooms this year, yet Cody still enjoyed ridiculing Calder whenever he thought he could get away with it. Cody Kenyon left the classroom after turning in a paper. He curled his lip and snickered as he passed, "Later, Scuzzball!"

Good riddance! thought Calder as he turned his attention to what was taking place at the front of the class. Mrs. Nicholas was dividing the students into groups of early humans.

"Can I be Homo-sapiens?" pleaded Joe.

"You're more like a Neanderthal!" laughed Derick, which caused a little chuckle. Joe was a broad football player, but he didn't mind Derick's comment; they were friends and often teased each other.

Calder moved forward. He liked social studies, but he also wanted to join in the silliness. "Can I be a *Crow Magma?*" he called, purposely mispronouncing the words *Cro Magnon*, and eliciting the reaction he was looking for, a few laughs and a few groans. Mrs. Nicholas told them to settle down and they all became more focused.

"Imagine going back in time about two million years to the plains of East Africa..." she began. Calder immediately imagined the dry heat of Africa, and could practically smell the beasts of the Savannah plain.

At the end of social studies the bell rang, the double doors opened, and the noisy students spilled out and scattered in all directions, like a broken pearl necklace on a marble floor. Calder and Derick grabbed their bikes and headed up the hill.

"Wait up!" called Joe as he ran to catch up. Derick and Joe had been able to see through Calder's court-jester persona. They had found him to be an interesting, funny, and loyal friend. Inspired by the social studies lesson, the three walked through the canyon searching for relics of an ancient past.

"Imagine going back two hundred years to the canyons of San Diego," began Calder pensively.

"Y'know, the Diegueno and Kumeyaay tribes really were indigenous to this area, way before the missionaries came to California," marveled Joe.

"You mean we really could find ancient treasures?" asked Derick.

"Yeah, fragments of terra-cotta pottery and flint arrowheads have already been unearthed, so I'd imagine there's more to be discovered," continued Joe. "We could go exploring this weekend if you like." They all liked the idea of becoming weekend archaeologists.

"Count me in," volunteered Calder.

Derick agreed, then changed the subject. "You guys going to the dance t'night?"

"Yeah, I'll be there," answered Joe.

"It'll be awesome!" I went last month and had a blast!" said Calder. I didn't dance, of course. I just stood around soaking up the vibes!"

"Cool, see ya there," Joe called as he headed down the street.

"Who's driving us there?" Calder asked Derick. "Your mom or mine?"

"Don't know! Call you when I get home, okay?"

"Okay, later!" said Calder, leaping onto his bike and continuing towards home.

Jenna offered to drive them to the dance as she could see the excitement oozing from every pore of Calder's soul.

"Everybody was Kung-Fu fighting, Diddle-iddle-ing ting-ting-ting-ting. Those cats were fast as lightnin'," he sang. Jenna was glad to see Calder in high spirits. He had his shower early because his long hair took a while to dry. He chose to wear his camouflage cargo pants, his black long-sleeved surfer shirt, and his cowry shell necklace. "It was a little bit frightenin'," he sang as he fought to gain control of his tangled mop of streaky blond hair.

Sarah, Jade, and Azule piled into the S.U.V. and headed to the mall with Sarah's mom driving. Sarah and Jade talked non-stop about *What to wear,* and *Who'll be there,* and *What's the latest dance?* Subjects that didn't usually enter Azule's mind, but it was fun to be involved in the excitement. The girls took a few dollars to spend, just enough for a new top or an inexpensive, but totally fashionable piece of jewelry. Azule found a leather cord necklace with an enameled *yin and yang* symbol dangling from a spiral loop. She tried it on and it hung in perfect balance, just below the hollow of her throat. "Cool!" she exclaimed, instantly satisfied. The other two girls took over an hour trying on the latest fashions, eventually settling on identical tops, each in a different color. Sarah chose pink and Jade chose turquoise.

At 6:30 Jenna dropped Calder and Derick off in the parking lot, and the boys made their way to the gate, where kids were lining up to show their I.D.s. A folded photocopy of their latest report card proved that they were sixth-graders.

"Y--M--C--A," the pulsing music boomed as the boys entered the hall, which was filled to capacity. The massive throng looked like a sea of bobbing, swaying, laughing, chatting adolescents -- all eager to meet and mingle, like an ocean of characters that ebbed and flowed to the music.

The noise was intense. Calder examined the crowd and picked out several faces that he recognized. He saw Azule and raised his chin in acknowledgement. Azule smiled back. She was standing with Sarah and Jade who both saw Calder, but pretended not to; they just looked away. Calder moved deeper into the throbbing crowd of dancers. He didn't dance his way through, he just let the pull of the wave guide him, like flotsam and jetsam, across the hall to where he had spotted Joe.

"Hey Dude, what's up?" greeted Joe in his California-cool style. He was leaning by the wall with one foot against it and his hands in the pockets of his long leather coat.

"Hey," replied Calder, "Derick's over here. We're getting pizza."

"I just ate at home," replied Joe, "but I'll come over anyway."

Calder saw Cody Kenyon staring his way, so he averted his eyes in order to avoid another confrontation; he was intent on enjoying his evening. He spotted Adam in the crowd and waved the *shaka* surfers' wave (little finger and thumb sticking out and a swiveling flick o' the wrist). Joe hadn't seen Adam since the photography class, so they greeted each other with a mutual nod and headed over towards Derick, who had found a few more friends. Now eight of them were swapping stories, eating pizza, sipping sodas, and keeping an eagle eye on the dance floor.

"Let's go talk to Joe," suggested Sarah, scanning the crowded scene.

"I thought you didn't like him," replied Jade sarcastically.

"Oh, Joe's pretty cool and he's with a big crowd of boys," Sarah argued convincingly. They persuaded Azule to join them as they danced across the floor. Sarah raised both arms above her head and squeezed through the crowd, smiling straight at Joe. "Do you always hang out at these sixth-grade dances?" she asked him.

"So far," he said coolly, being careful to remain aloof.

Calder would have said "Hi" to all of them, but Jade and

Sarah were otherwise engaged, trying to impress Joe and Adam. "Rad necklace," he complimented Azule.

"Yin and yang," she said, pulling it up and trying to examine it. "It symbolizes dualities, like black and white, day and night, wrong and right, y'know," she added.

"Hmm, very interesting," he said, stroking his chin like a mad scientist. For the moment he was running out of things to say. "V-err-ee in-ter-est-ing!" he repeated. "Hey, do y'wanna dance?"

Azule laughed and said, "No thanks, Calder."

Calder laughed too, "I was hoping you'd say that." He went on to divulge that the *Yin* symbolized the feminine, and the *Yang* symbolized the masculine. "It's the Daoist symbol for dualities and balance," he continued. "Lao-zi believed we should be in harmony with nature."

"You're just bubbling over with obscure trivia, aren't you?" she chuckled. Calder felt comfortable with Azule, because like him, she was a collector of random knowledge.

The dance came to an end and after most kids had been picked up, Calder realized that Cody was heading his way with a menacing look in his eyes.

"This dude has a major anger problem," said Calder. "Let's split!" But it was too late. Before Calder could move, Cody's fist had landed squarely on the bridge of his nose. Calder reeled backwards into Joe. The attack took them both by surprise, but Joe was able to regain his equilibrium. Grabbing Cody by the collar he snarled, "What's your problem, Dude?" Then he pushed Cody away from Calder, who was crumpled in a heap against the wall.

Just then the headlights of Jenna's car froze the sorry scene and Cody ran off yelling, "I'm gonna kick your skinny butt, Caveman!" Joe helped Calder to his feet and into the car, explaining to Jenna what had just happened.

The weekend came and went without the boys ever getting together for their archaeological exploration. Calder's mom had whisked him straight to the emergency room. His nose was bruised, but not broken; shaken, not stirred! Calder's baseball game had dominated Saturday's events, but although Calder tried to show team spirit he really wasn't into it, his nose hurt and he had a bit of a black eye.

Sunday morning, Calder was feeling better, but still frustrated with Cody Kenyon, so he grabbed his board and headed for the beach at Cardiff Reef to clear his head. Paddling out, he felt the tension washing away from his body. The sky was cobalt blue and the waves perfect. Joe and Dave were already out riding a slick wave. Calder waved a *shaka* greeting towards the brothers, but then he headed farther south, in need of space.

As he caught one wave after another he began to tune in to the rhythm. With the cool spray in his face and the exhilarating descent down the wall of the wave, his frustrations at last began to dissipate; once again he was in harmony with nature! After all, Cody was the one who had a problem. Why should Calder waste time and energy on someone else's anger?

A huge set rolled in. Calder waited for the mega wave, the Tsunami! But he messed up, went over the falls, and got sucked into the *washing machine*, rolling and tumbling against the pebbles on the ocean floor. POUNDED! He held his breath, but his lungs were burning. Looking skyward, Calder kicked with all his might, but the wave was powerful, held him down a moment longer, rolled him again, then spit him out right in front of Joe. He shook his head and flicked his wet hair back, choking and gasping for air as salt water gushed from every orifice. Yet Calder was bubbling over with exhilaration.

"Whoa, that was totally Rad, Dude," he screamed. "Let's go catch another!" Life was good again!

Azule was an avid writer. That same weekend she had decided to advance her skills by creating a sixth-grade magazine. She discussed it with some of her more literary friends and by Monday they were chatting excitedly about the prospects of a *News Page, Chat Column, Essay Contest,* and a monthly puzzle or brain-teaser.

"What shall we call our magazine?" Azule asked.

"Hmm, how about *The Infernal Journal?*" giggled Maddy.

"What about *The Surf n' Turf,* like the racetrack?" offered Ellie.

"Or *Kids Gigs?*" Sarah joined in.

"Yeah, but we aren't kids anymore, we're *Pre-teens,*" said Ellie with an imperious air of pride. They were sitting on the steps of the newly-scored playing field. The sun was hot, but not scorching as they huddled together, braiding hair and brainstorming over their new creation.

Finally Azule announced, "*Solar Flare!*" Apparently the sun had seared a good idea into her brain and they all eagerly agreed upon it; the *Sixth Grade Solar Flare* it would be! A bi-monthly magazine full of interesting snips, submitted by any sixth-grader.

"Let's ask our parents if they'd be willing to donate prizes," suggested Jade.

"Gift certificates to the movie-theater or video store would be good," recommended Sarah. Azule eagerly made notes of everyone's suggestions.

After school, Azule found Calder standing by the bike rack waiting for Derick. Ellie had already told her what Cody had done after the dance, so she was careful not to mention his fat nose and his black eye. Instead, she asked Calder if he would be interested in submitting some of his drawings to her magazine.

"What bagazine?" he muttered through his fat, swollen nose. Azule stifled a giggle, then explained her idea. She had seen his artwork during the summer camp and had been impressed. His sketches of medieval castles, hawks, and knights, were quite detailed. Calder shrugged and said he didn't think his drawings were good enough.

"You've got to be kidding, Calder," Azule reassured him. "Your drawings are so cool!"

Then Derick arrived on the scene, so Calder replied, "Okay -- sure -- maybe."

Azule thought it best to leave it at that, so she said a meager "Hi" to Derick, then left to catch up with Ellie. The boys ambled aimlessly through the canyon, discussing the possibilities of time-traveling to a different era. Derick decided that his preferred era would be Roman times; he fancied himself as a gladiator or a charioteer.

Calder hesitated for a moment, then once again confided to Derick that he'd already experienced life in medieval England first-hand. "Yeah, I'm not joking, I think I slipped through a time warp into a parallel era or something! Not once, but thrice!"

Derick just laughed out loud and said, "Wow! That's just insane, Dude! That thump on the nose must have shaken your senses. Earth to Calder -- Earth to Calder..."

A Tale of Two Calders

That night Calder studied his sketches and reminisced about his visits to England. A year ago, on his last trip to visit his nana, he'd had a most peculiar experience which, in effect, had turned his perception of reality inside out and had set his numerous space/time theories in motion. He clearly remembered how the first time-warp had happened:

The village of Thornhill was small and ancient, yet full of character, sitting on top of a long triangular plateau. At the bottom of the craggy south-facing ridge, the pasture sloped gently down to a winding stream edged with ancient oak trees and hawthorn hedges, where four fields converged onto a secluded wooden bridge, half-hidden by ferns and nettles.

Calder was running down the steep, craggy hill. At the bottom of the hill he found an old stone stile and looked up at a metal signpost. The lettering was barely legible, eroded by rust over the centuries. He strained to decipher the words, **Public Footpath**. Placing one foot on the iron crossbar and gripping the post, he pulled himself onto the stone stile, where he was high enough to see over the hedge into the neighboring field. Calder whistled. A great thundering of hooves grew closer, then suddenly a magnificent equine head appeared over the hawthorn hedge. Warm, steamy air blasted from the horse's wide nostrils as he shook his mane and whinnied at Calder's beaming face. The horse seemed to smile back, his big black sparkling eyes glinting like polished ebony jaw-breakers.

Calder reached into his pocket and pulled out a small apple that he'd taken from his nana's fruit bowl. He felt the soft hair and skin of the horse's muzzle as it gently pulled the apple from his open hand and chomped it. Calder looked into the horse's huge black eye and saw his own reflection staring back, but he didn't see the bronzed California kid standing there, he saw himself as a young knight in shining armor. There goes my tournament charger, he thought as the horse took off. "I name thee Gallahad!" But the horse cared nothing for names and galloped freely around the field, his coat gleaming in the sunlight, black and shiny like coal. He had a long dark mane and a white diamond on his forehead.

Calder felt the earth tremble under the weight of Gallahad's massive hooves and imagined how brilliant it would be to ride such a magnificent beast in a medieval jousting tournament. He watched as Gallahad did something Calder had never seen a horse do before. At the top of the field, Gallahad rolled on his back with glee and kicked his hooves in the air. A wonderful sight!

Calder felt privileged to have seen such mirth in a creature; it made him appreciate life even more than he *already did.* He leaped from the stile and ran down the winding dirt path, which led to the ancient wooden bridge of Smithy Brook. Calder loved to play under the bridge; it smelled of mushrooms and medieval times. Creeping below, with the stream rushing by, he imagined the Billy-goat's hooves clip-clopping on the old Troll bridge above his head. *Who's that stepping on my bridge....?* he thought as a shudder ran down his spine. It was way too creepy being under there alone, so Calder made his way back up the hill to his nana's house.

The following day, carrying a bag of sliced apples, Calder had gone in search of his noble Gallahad. He whistled, but this time there had been no sign of the massive cart-horse. *But here are some takers,* thought Calder, noticing a herd of white ponies in the adjacent field. From a distance they looked small and tame, but when two of them approached, Calder realized that their backs were higher than his shoulder.

He held out a piece of apple to one pony and reached into the bag to offer a wedge to the second, but being slightly apprehensive, Calder had fumbled and dropped it. To his astonishment the larger pony became quite agitated and bit the other pony on the neck as it reached down for the apple. Then, thud -- thud -- thud, it turned and kicked at its flanks.

"Stop, stop!" cried Calder. "There's plenty for both of you." But, thud -- thud -- thud, the pony kicked again. Finally, the smaller one turned and bolted, but now several other ponies were heading his way and the situation was reeling out of control. There was no fence between Calder and the ponies, and the aggressor was nudging him for more apples. What if it tried to kick him when he ran out of treats, and what would happen when the rest of the herd arrived?

For a quick getaway, Calder threw the apple pieces to the ground in front of the malcontent and ran as fast as he could. Up the footpath, over the stile, along the lane, scrambling back up the craggy ridge to where his nana's house used to be... *Used to be?* he thought as he looked at the empty dirt lane. "Where's my nana's red brick bungalow gone?" Calder gasped.

It was then that he realized something truly unusual had happened. *Perhaps,* he pondered, *perhaps I **was** kicked in the head by that irate pony and I'm having a concussive nightmare?* But this was no nightmare, this was fun, and peaceful, and very exciting.

The wind was beginning to blow, laced with just a few drops of rain. As Calder ran, his memory of the twenty-first century faded, until he had no recollection of it whatsoever; he was just an eleven-year-old youth running through the village of Thornhill. It was the **fifteenth** century! In his belt he carried a wooden sword; he was Calder, the medieval Knight-in-Training. He wore a chestnut-brown woolen tunic over his long-sleeved cream shirt. He stopped for a moment to pull up his loose-fitting leggings and to fasten the laces of his soft brown leather ankle boots. Then he set off again at a more leisurely pace, pulling his sword from his belt and merrily stabbing at the tangled brambles of a blackberry bush.

"Take that, ye Dastardly Dragon!" he laughed. Dark purple/red juice spattered everywhere, making him jump back to avoid staining his tunic.

As Calder reached the edge of Thornhill, the Tang -- Tang -- Tang of the blacksmith's heavy metal hammer could be heard, pounding the anvil in the forge-yard, where a pillar of black smoke rose into the drizzle-gray sky.

Mr. Bradford looked up. "Killed ye mighty dragon, yet Lad?" he asked.

"Aye, that I have," Calder shouted back. He waved his sword, showing the haematic stains of blackberry juice upon it. Mr. Bradford let out a hearty laugh, then the Tang -- Tang -- Tang resumed, echoing across the valley behind Calder.

He headed north to the village center, then east down a narrow dirt passageway known as the ginnel, leading to Kirkfield (the field adjacent to the church). Both had been there since at least the thirteenth century. Unbeknown to Calder, the church, the ginnel, and Kirkfield would still be there in the twenty-first century. And so perhaps, would he!

"Hey Calder, dost thou want to laik?" called out a youthful voice from the field.

"What art thou laikin', Hugo?" asked Calder. He wasn't surprised to see his friend playing in Kirkfield, which was filled with row upon row of huge rolled bales of hay, as high as the top of their heads.

"We're laikin' at knights and dragons!" announced Hugo.

Another boy leaped out from behind a bale of hay. "And I be Sir Bedevere," he shouted. It was Thomas and he was wearing a wooden pail on his head. The two young knights laughed, stabbing fiercely at the bales of hay.

"I dare thee, evil dragon, to breathe one flicker of thy fiery breath in my direction," yelled Calder, slashing at the drizzly air and broad-siding the haystack with his berry-stained wooden sword.

After a while the boys abandoned the dragon game.

Hugo kicked an inflated pig-bladder ball towards Calder. Thomas intercepted. Calder tackled Thomas , then passed it back to Hugo, who carefully aimed for the space between the two hay stacks and scored a goal. Little did they know, they had invented soccer several centuries ahead of its time. But soon the drops of rain became puddles of rain and the wind began to blow stronger, throwing slivers of straw up all around them. A tiding of magpies circled overhead calling out their warnings that sounded like, Quick -- Quick -- Quick. Calder counted them: One for sorrow, two for joy, three for a girl, four for a boy, five for silver, six for gold, seven for a secret never to be told!

He ran through the graveyard and out through an ornate wooden portal on the east side of the churchyard. Hugo and Thomas followed close behind, across the muddy street, over the low stone wall, and between the young oak trees to where Calder's cottage stood. His mother, Gwenna was bringing in her laundered sheets, which seemed to be flapping like huge sails on the high seas.

"Beware, a storm is brewing, lads," she called after them, but the boys didn't stop. They just kept on running, brandishing their swords high above their heads, to where the hill dropped steeply away on the eastern edge of Thornhill. The three young knights stood motionless at the top of the hill, surveying the land below.

Calder looked down to where the new manor was being built on the property that had once belonged to his ancestor, Sir John de Thornhill. In the late 1300's, Sir John's granddaughter, Elizabeth, had married Sir Henry Savile. The noble Saviles now owned the land and the new manor house.

"There be much chaos here this day," remarked Hugo,

noticing a newly-trenched moat around the central island. Water was being siphoned into it from the ponds behind the adjacent farm.

"Aye, but should they wait a while, the rainwater might flow down yonder hill and fill the moat this very night," sighed Calder. "Methinks, water always seeketh the lowest point." By now the rain was coming down in big globs, the wind whipped around their legs, and the storm was advancing ever closer.

"Let us venture home, for I be chilled to the bone and I need ye dragon's fiery breath to warm me," laughed Thomas, turning into the wind. At Calder's cottage they split up; Hugo and Thomas headed towards the village as Calder entered his timbered cottage.

"Where hast thou been, Son?" asked Calder's mother.

"Just laiking," answered Calder. "Training to be a knight with my goodfellows, Hugo and Thomas, but if I am to be a knight, I must procure a finer sword than this," he said discarding his outgrown weapon.

"Ah, thou wilt make a good knight like thy brother, Sir Jordan, and my great, great-grandfather, Sir John," Gwenna cooed. Calder's brother was twenty-four and already a knight at Sandal castle, in the city of Wakefield. "But now thou must feed the hens and goats, my good Sir Calder!"

The young, wannabe knight scooped a ladleful of grain along with a pail of alfalfa and ran outside to scatter it amongst the chickens and goats. He picked up a small mouse, which the cat had apparently killed and slipped it into his leather pouch, then went to the outer-house where he kept his kestrel. Calder pulled on his leather gauntlet and held out his hand at shoulder height. Jack swooped down from his lofty perch and landed deftly on Calder's glove, sinking his sharp talons into the thick leather. He eyed his master intently. Holding the kestrel's leather jesses between his fingers, Calder secured the hawk and took him outside.

"Soar high, my good fellow," willed Calder as he released Jack, but he didn't plan to let him fly for long because the storm was imminent. Calder watched Jack hovering as though suspended from some invisible wire, a dark speck silhouetted against the moody sky. Suddenly the hawk swooped down, picked up a rodent from the ground, and flew back into the trees. Calder had observed this behavior on numerous occasions. Jack had become his wild pet two years earlier when he found the young fledgling with an injured wing and Calder had repaired it with a splint. Although he thought it best to keep him safe in the loft, Calder set Jack free as often as he could.

After ten minutes, Calder whistled his high-pitched call and Jack returned to his outstretched gauntlet. Pinched between the leather thumb and forefinger was the offering of the mouse, which the hawk tore with its razor-sharp beak. Being a raptor, he preferred to catch his own live prey, but wouldn't refuse a freshly killed mouse when one was offered. Jack returned to his perch and settled with an ever watchful eye.

Calder removed his gauntlet and went back inside. The sky was turning a deep shade of indigo, and moments later a more serious rain pelted the tiny window panes. Gwenna was preparing rabbit stew for dinner. She turned as Calder entered, flicked her long auburn braid down her back, straightened her apron over her green linen dress, and continued chopping vegetables to add to the broth in the iron pot.

Calder was stoking the fire in the hearth when his father arrived. William was a constable in the city of Wakefield. He was a tall, important-looking, gentle man with blond hair curling onto his broad shoulders. He had ridden home in the rain, so his face was ruddy and wet. He stood in the entrance and took off his hat and cloak, then hung them on an iron peg behind the oak door. He kissed Gwenna gently on the cheek, carried the heavy cauldron of stew to the hook above the blazing fire, then sat in the chair next to the warm fireplace. Calder stood up and helped his father take off his wet boots, carefully placing them on the edge of the flagstone hearth to dry.

"Art thou warmer now, Father?" he asked.

"Aye, considerably warmer thanks to thee, Son," was his father's grateful reply. He rubbed his cold hands together and felt the fire's warmth, then turned and smiled affectionately at Gwenna, glad to be home.

"Father, prithee wilt thou inquire at the castle that I might join Sir Jordan in training to be a knight? I am now almost twelve years of age and children's games no longer interest me."

"Aye Son, thou art truly a young man of great fortitude and honor, but thou hast yet some growing to do before becoming a knight," replied William, patting Calder on his shoulder. "However, I will speak to Lord Savile and put in a good word for thee." Calder was satisfied that he had been taken seriously. It was now up to him to study and practice the ways of a knight.

About an hour later, there was a gentle rapping on the doorknocker. Calder looked towards his father, who nodded to him to open the door. Lifting the iron latch, he found a pair of bedraggled figures standing in the wild, wet weather.

"Ah, prithee enter!" announced Calder, welcoming his Aunt Catherine and cousin Abigail into the house. "Thou art just in time for some heart-warming rabbit stew."

"That sounds pleasurable this foul night," replied his aunt, shaking off the rain. There was always plenty of good food at Calder's house, and family was always welcome. William carried the steaming pot from the hook above the fire, back to the long wooden table. Calder took their visitors' cloaks and hung them to dry behind the door. He was happy to have company, especially cousin Abigail, who was his age and shared similar interests. As the family sat down to eat and chat about their day's events, Gwenna provided more bowls, spoons, and another loaf of crusty bread.

After dinner the two cousins played marbles on the living room floor, while the adults talked incessantly. The glowing fire lit the room as well as warming it, but the flagstone floor was cold, so Calder gave Abigail a needlepoint cushion to sit upon, and he placed a beeswax candle at her side. Abigail blushed and thanked her cousin.

In an attempt to entertain, Calder linked his thumbs and spread his fingers above the flickering candle flame, casting a shadow of a bird in flight across the ceiling. Abigail giggled gleefully at Calder's creative prank, and although he was quite tired after his long day of slaying dragons, their game of marbles and their parents' conversations went on until quite late.

"Fare thee well and many thanks to thee," said Aunt Catherine, as she and Abigail finally stepped outside into the perpetually pouring rain.

"Hugo, Thomas, and I plan to laik at Kirkfield on the morrow," Calder called to Abigail. "Prithee, come with us if thou liketh."

"Aye, I will do so, if 'tis not raining so," laughed Abigail, pulling her hood down over her forehead to brave the weather. She did enjoy playing Guinevere, when Calder, Hugo, and Thomas were playing the Knights of the Round Table. "Sleep well and may'st thou have sweet dreams," she called.

Calder came back into the warmth of his home. The embers of the fire were still glowing red as the flickering shadows moved across the ceiling. He snuffed the candle, raked the embers, and called out, "Good night" to his parents, who were already retiring to their chamber at the back of the house. He took off his tunic, cleaned his teeth with a frayed piece of dried licorice root, and fell backwards onto his horse-hair mattress in the far curtained corner of the living room. It was far more comfortable than his old straw mattress had been.

Calder, the soon-to-be medieval knight-in-training, looked up at the timbered ceiling. His tired eyes traced the decorative white frieze of plastered acorns and oak leaves, which graced the upper edges of the four walls. He pulled his woolen blanket up around his shoulders and listened to the soothing sound of heavy rain falling on the slate roof, as it lulled him gently into a deep sleep.

He was totally oblivious to the notion that another Calder from the future millennium, the twenty-first century, had somehow slipped through a time warp, and had been experiencing medieval Calder's life that very day.

Into the Belly of the Beast

Calder awoke at his nana's house the next morning and looked up at the ceiling. It was plain white plaster and the walls were wallpapered. He wasn't in the medieval timbered house any more, he was in the bungalow. Diagonal shafts of light streamed across the tiny bedroom through the blinds. He couldn't remember what had happened in the horse pasture that could have caused him to experience the medieval world. All he remembered was coming back up the hill towards his nana's bungalow. From then on he'd been in a different era.

"What did we do last night, Nana?" he asked as he stretched and made his way to the bathroom.

"Well," she began, "we had sausage, mash, and peas. Then we watched a film about Robin Hood, didn't we?"

"Oh yeah," he said, "now I remember." He actually thought he did remember, but it seemed like such a long time ago. So, what on earth had happened? He decided he must go out and explore Thornhill to see if he could find any relic from the past, any trace of evidence from what he had experienced the previous day. Could there possibly be anything remaining in the village after more than five centuries?

"Is there a moat somewhere near the church, Nana?" he inquired.

"Yes, Love, your mum used to play down there when she was a girl. It's across from the church, around the ruins of old Thornhill Hall," replied his nana. "We took you there when you were little."

Calder remembered a photo of himself in the album at home; a little blond haired two-year-old sitting high upon a stone wall. He was wearing a silver plastic chest-plate and helmet, and was brandishing a plastic sword. He wondered if that had been the occasion.

"Yes, that was it," said Nana.

"We can walk down there later if you want to," interjected Jenna. "It's not far, and it's steeped in history."

"Can I go there on my own?" pleaded Calder. "I'm old enough!"

"Well, why not ask Dave if he'd like to go with you," Jenna suggested. "He probably knows all the cool hideouts." Dave was Jenna's friend's son. He was a little older than Calder and had grown up in Thornhill. "But stay together," she cautioned. "You're safer exploring in twos."

After breakfast, Calder ran to Dave's house. The houses in the neighborhood were certainly too new to have been there in the Middle Ages. Calder tried to figure out the lay of the land. Hmm, I recognize this area; it was open heath back in Hugo's day, he thought, as he crossed the park to where his friend's Edwardian house stood. Dave was glad to go exploring with Calder, so they headed east towards the church.

"Shall we cut through the graveyard?" asked Calder.

"D' you dare?" replied Dave.

"I've been there before!" boasted Calder.

"Oh aye, when was that, you've only been in England a few days?"

"Oh, it was a long, long time ago," laughed Calder. "Centuries ago!"

There was an estate of new houses on the way to Kirkfield, but the narrow passageway (the ginnel), still existed. It ran between two houses, and led to the field where medieval Calder had played with Hugo and Thomas. As tradition would have it, there were some huge rolled bales of hay in Kirkfield, just as there had been over five hundred years earlier. Everything began to look familiar. The boys ran down to the church, just as medieval Calder had done with Hugo and Thomas, but these days the church remained locked (except Sundays) due to recent vandalism in the area. Nothing's sacred anymore, thought Calder.

The boys searched through the graveyard. Calder said he wanted to find the oldest grave, but really he was searching for his medieval friends. They had found many prominent gravestones from the 1700's and even a few from the 1600's, when Dave remembered there were some even older ones around the back of the church. At that moment Calder had a spooky thought: What if he found his own grave? Aaaargh! He shuddered and gasped, "Nah! let's go to the moat." They ran through the timbered Lych-gate (now blackened with age, but just as ornately beautiful as before.)

Calder jumped over the low stone wall and looked at

the place where medieval Calder's cottage would have stood. The young oaks that had surrounded it were still there, but they were now great gnarled oak trees, and his cottage was long gone. In its place was a mini-golf putting green. They ran to the edge of the hill, where Calder had previously looked down towards old the manor.

He took a deep breath and ran full speed down the slope to the edge of the moat, with Dave following close behind. The moat was covered with a layer of green duckweed, making it look more like a lawn. A bicycle wheel was sticking out of the water and a detergent box protruded at an angle, its orange and red commercial logo looking quite incongruous in such a historical setting. The moat wasn't as deep as it had been back in medieval times. Over the centuries all kinds of junk had found its way in there. Calder sighed in disgust.

In the late 1400's there had been the new manor. Now, all that stood before him were the ruins. Facing him, across the moat on the central island, were two stone pedestals. Each had a ghostly headless form crouching upon it. Between the eroded figures, several granite steps led down to the murky moat.

"Spo-o-o-o-ky!" croaked Calder hypnotically, remembering how he and his friends had admired the new manor in the fifteenth century. It had been quite a magnificent entrance, even before the gate posts had been built.

"Those white relics were once a pair o' marble griffins, Gog and Magog, the guardians of the manor," Dave divulged.

"But now they're reduced to these two ghoulish blobs," sighed Calder.

"Yeah, Blob and Mablob, the guardians o' the rubble," snickered Dave mischievously.

"Great security system," mused Calder, "but what happened to the manor house in the end?"

"It burned to t' ground in 1648 when there was civil unrest in England," Dave explained. "Half the country supported the King and t' other half supported Parliament. The Saviles were Royalists, but Fairfax's men had 'em surrounded. After a bit of a stand-off, fighting broke out and somehow, so the story goes, their own gunpowder ignited inside the house and burned it down. All were killed or severely burned," Dave continued. "Highly suspicious, if y' ask me."

"Wow, did you learn all that in school, Dave?" asked Calder, impressed with his knowledge.

"No, the Historical Society re-enacts it every few years. It's great! You should come to t' next one, if you're 'ere," Dave invited. "C'mon, I'll show you the way across to the old manor," he added, running around the left side of the moat and through a broken-down fence, overgrown with weeds and nettles. Calder wasn't familiar with nettles and stepped right into them.

"Ouch my legs are totally itchy!" he complained.

Dave reached for a large dock leaf. "Ere, rub this on it," he said. "The antidote grows right next to t' nettles."

"This guy's a walking almanac!" exclaimed Calder, feeling less itchy already. "Dude, you're amazing!" he added appreciatively.

As they crossed the rickety bridge Dave asked, "Did you hear about t' lad who drowned in this moat centuries ago?"

"No," answered Calder. "So, is it haunted?" He looked

down into the water and thought of the poor boy. He felt like he'd heard enough for one day, so he didn't pursue it any further and Dave didn't answer.

The boys stood on the island, which had been reclaimed by trees, birds, and brambles. They stopped in their tracks near the huge derelict fireplace, scrawled with graffiti. Below that, sat two boys about their own age, drinking something from a bottle in a brown paper bag; they appeared to be smoking cigarettes too.

"Let's get outta 'ere," whispered Dave, in case there was trouble.

"No respect for the past," muttered Calder turning away. He wanted to give them a piece of his mind, but decided not to get into an altercation.

"Ey-up, Yank, come ovver 'ere!" shouted the drunken punks in their strong Yorkshire accents. They had recognized Calder's American twang.

Dave and Calder turned on their heels and scarpered fast down the dip, avoiding the nettles. Over the fence, across the park, past the swings, and up the very steep slope to the flat golf area, where medieval Calder's cottage had been. Calder stopped and leaned against one of the great oaks to catch his breath. A rustling sound in the leaves at the base of the tree startled him.

"The drowned boy's ghost!" whispered Dave and they both laughed heartily. Then out from under the dried leaves scurried a prickly hedgehog. Calder had never seen one before, so he was elated.

"It looks like a tiny porcupine with a pointed twitchy black nose," he observed.

"Looks more like a mucky toilet brush on legs!" laughed Dave. "Where d' ya wanna go next, Yank?"

"D'you know where the market cross is?" asked Calder eagerly.

Dave led the way to what was now simply known as the Cross. As they walked, Calder realized that he could easily have found his way there; the layout hadn't changed at all in over five centuries. They came to the crooked crossroads in the heart of the village. The ancient cross was still there, but all that remained of it was a stumpy pedestal of stone and the water trough. The cross had been erected by Sir John de Thornhill, when he created the marketplace in 1317. A Victorian gas lamp stood next to the village relics.

"This was added later, much later," remarked Calder looking at the nineteenth century monument.

"I've lived 'ere my 'ole life and I've never really noticed that. How come you know s' much about it, Calder?" asked Dave, now full of curiosity. Calder was tempted to tell Dave the whole story, but was afraid Dave would think him crazy, so he said, "I know many things, Man!"

Looking around, Calder imagined the medieval village, alive with the hustle and bustle of market day, but the Cross was now just a quiet junction in the middle of nowhere. The village had long ago become a suburb of a larger industrial town.

Calder picked up a twig from the dry stone trough and swished it in the air like a sword as they walked towards the park.

"D' ya wanna go down to the stream and the old Troll bridge?" asked Calder.

"Oh, you mean t' beck? Aye, let's go!" said Dave eagerly. So they set off across the park, heading south towards the craggy ridge where Calder had been the previous day when the time warp had first occurred. From there, they looked across the valley. A tall television tower dominated the horizon. To the left of that, Dave pointed out the shaft-tower of a mining museum, and spread in front of them like a huge soft green velvet patchwork quilt, lay the valley with its irregular shaped fields, separated by black stone walls, oak trees, and hawthorn hedges. Calder's eyes followed the meandering stream to the area where four fields converged on the Troll bridge.

"Race you down to t' beck," prompted Dave. By now Calder realized that "beck" was the old Yorkshire word for stream. Some things definitely hadn't changed.

"You're on!" said Calder racing and stumbling down the craggy ridge. At the stile near the horse's field, Calder hesitated. He didn't want any trouble with the ponies today. Luckily they were gone. Dave showed Calder a hidden rope-swing that hung from the branch of the great oak. They played for about an hour, swinging over the stream and running over the bridge. Growling stomachs eventually made them realize that they hadn't eaten at all since breakfast and it was now mid-afternoon, so they trudged wearily back up the craggy hill to Nana's bungalow.

"I'm sure you can stay for tea," offered Calder.

"Good! 'Cos I could eat a scabby donkey slapped between two bread bins!" exaggerated Dave, as they dragged their weary legs back up the long dirt path with blackberry bushes on either side.

This was where I became a dragon-slayer, thought Calder, half expecting to hear the Tang -- Tang -- Tang of Mr. Bradford's hammer striking the anvil. He looked skyward and saw a small speck hovering, but the trill song told him that it was a skylark, not a kestrel. He thought of

Jack and wondered if any kestrels had survived into the twenty-first century.

"How would you boys like to go four-hundred-twenty-five feet down a mine shaft tomorrow?" Jenna asked as they entered Nana's house.

"Sounds awesome!" said Calder.

"Cool!" mimicked Dave. He was happy to see that his mom had arrived, so he didn't have to cross Thornhill again on foot.

"These boys look like they've had a full day of adventure," remarked Nana, putting the kettle on for a welcome cup of tea and fussing over a plate of egg salad sandwiches. They devoured the food in silence, offering no details of their day's events.

Calder was invited to spend the night at Dave's house. In their living room, there was a billiard table and two large leather Chesterfield couches. Dave taught Calder the basic rules of billiards and the boys laughed and played for hours. When they could concentrate no longer, they each rolled out a sleeping bag on the comfy couches and watched the last glowing embers of the log fire in the fireplace. Just like medieval times, thought Calder as he slipped into a dream.

Calder felt as though he was descending the throat of a dragon after being swallowed whole. He shuddered. Down, down, and deeper went the cage into the belly of the beast. But this was no dream, this was really happening. It was the next day and he was inside a cage with Dave, their moms, six other people, and the mining museum tour guide. Nana had stayed on the surface, since she didn't like the idea of being so far below ground.

Through the elevator cage, Calder could see water trickling steadily down the mossy brick sides of the pit shaft. Darker, damper, and colder it became until the cage reached the bottom with a shudder. Everyone was wearing a hard hat and a battery pack with flashlights attached. They wore them around their necks, the way a doctor would wear a stethoscope, so as not to shine the light in anyone else's eyes.

The lift gate clanked open and the tour began: "Ole fam'lies lived below ground and worked t'gether on t' coal seam. Their lives wor really miserable! Toddlers wor attached by a leash to their mothers, to stop 'em roaming off in t' pitch dark. Their only light wor a cangle, one cangle per family," rambled the guide. Calder giggled to himself because he knew the guide meant a candle. Earlier he had spoken of forty-five degree andles, when he obviously meant angles. "This guy doesn't know 'is angles from 'is cangles," snickered Calder under his breath, but then became more serious as he thought of those poor, wretched families underground.

"That wor in t' early nineteenth century, afore child labor wor abolished," continued the guide in his strong Yorkshire accent. Calder listened attentively and shuddered at the thought. "Ponies wor kept down t' mines to move t' wagons o' coal along," the guide persevered in his choppy dialect. "T' ponies wor treated better than t' people, 'cause unfortunately, t' people wor easier to replace."

Calder felt claustrophobic and wanted to go back up to the surface, but had to stay for the duration. He looked at the museum models of the mining families: Children blackened with coal dust, with barely any clothes to warm them. Mothers with heavy coal-carrying baskets strapped to their frail bony backs, crawling on their hands and knees. *This is every bit as bad as slavery,* thought Calder in disgust.

The rest of the tour was more technical, showing Davy lamps, coal-cutting machines, jack-hammers, and conveyer belts. Technology that spanned the centuries. Calder had enjoyed the tour, but breathed a sigh of relief when he reached the surface and had seen his nana waiting for them.

This trip to England and his first unexplained time-warp had all happened a year ago! And now, as Calder sat at his desk in his California bedroom recollecting those strange adventures, he had a decision to make: Whether or not he should submit his time-warp story and his drawing of a knight to Azule's sixth-grade magazine?

He realized that the cogs were once again in motion. Weird *time-warp* moments had started to happen in the photography class, just as they had in England a year ago. He needed to figure out how to take control of this phenomenon, how to learn to travel at will, and how to convince Derick and Joe that time-travel was not only possible, but plausible!

Feverishly he began typing. Spilling his medieval adventures into Microsoft Word.

Eye of Horus

Azule could see that Calder's personality would better suit a different era. His thinking was different and that intrigued her. He was forever talking about medieval times, or postulating how time-travel was possible. She was hoping that he would submit his drawing of a knight for their first edition of the *Sixth Grade Solar Flare*.

Azule decided to announce that she, Madeleine, and Ellie would be accepting essays and sketches for the first issue. Sarah and Jade were in charge of printing and circulation. They needed a crossword designer, a few jokes, and a list of suitable website addresses. They set a deadline of three weeks, as they knew everyone had book reports and map tests coming up.

Calder had been working on some detailed drawings; he thought he had the perspective right. One was a composition of a Norman helmet perched upon a rocky outcrop, a chestnut-colored horse grazing behind the helmet, and a shield with an interesting owl crest, leaning against the rock. The main subject was a young medieval knight wearing a red velvet cloak. A kestrel was perched on his gauntlet, and in the distance stood a majestic castle.

Calder pondered his medieval memories often. He realized that when he was in the twenty-first century he could remember everything about his fifteenth century experiences, but not vice-versa. When he was in medieval Thornhill he had no idea about the future, except for one time, when he played *Cotton Eye Joe* on his flute and couldn't figure out where he'd heard that tune. Come to think of it, nor could anyone else. They just said, "That be mighty fine playing, Calder!"

How was I able to slip through time into the past? Perhaps events lay side by side like folds in the cloth, or like the cluster of bubbles. Perhaps eras ran hand in hand like parallel universes, or like a *Moebius* strip, back to back. One totally unaware of the other, each twisting into a never-ending figure-of-eight. Calder didn't know the answer, but there certainly was no time machine, nor was there any magic floo powder in his experience!

He was trying to figure out his *Modus Travelendi* when Azule came into the room.

"How's your drawing coming along?" she inquired. Before he could answer, she saw it on the desk in front of him. "Wow," she said, "I like it! This is your best yet!" Calder had tried to slip the sketch under his earth science book, but the drawing was protruding on the side and she could see the horse and shield.

"May I see all of it?" Azule asked politely.

"Okay," Calder squirmed uneasily, but Azule was genuinely impressed so he began to feel more at ease.

When she asked about the location, Calder reluctantly began unraveling the tale about his adventures in England. She wasn't sure what was fact or which parts fantasy, but as usual she listened attentively. He told her about the helmet and how he had spent all his vacation money on it. She had seen the helmet during the summer photography class, but hadn't realized how important it was to Calder.

Madeleine and Ellie walked in at that moment and made their way over to Azule and Calder. They saw the drawing and were quite impressed, but Calder began to feel uncomfortable amongst so many girls. Maddy and Ellie thought Calder was okay, when he wasn't bubbling over with his crazy antics, but at that precise moment the court-jester persona resurfaced and Calder started rattling off some zany story about gremlins falling off cliffs. He danced around, waving his arms wildly as he mumbled, "Ogga-Bogga, save the *Grems* from their piteous extinction!"

After recess, the bell rang and the sixth-graders filed slowly back into the classroom for social studies. The subject of the day was Egyptology. They had *Egypt Day* planned for later in the month, when they would all dress in costumes and sample Egyptian food. Calder had several artifacts at home: a stone mummy known as a *shabti*, two statues of *Bast*, and a carved soapstone scarab beetle. He had a wide range of knowledge and his mind was chock full of interesting facts, if only he would share them. He chose instead to hide behind a whacky persona. This was his armor, his pseudo-self that protected him from being hurt, or from being known for that matter; it kept people at a safe distance.

"... Egyptology." the teacher ended her sentence, but

Calder had missed the whole introduction except for the last word. He had been daydreaming again, lost in his reveries of Thornhill, no doubt. Calder pulled his focus back to the present and looked over at his neighbor's desk to see what page they were on: Page one-hundred-eighty-four, *Ancient Egypt.*

He was quickly drawn into the illustrations of pyramids, papyrus, and the tomb of King Tutankhamen. His family had stayed at the Luxor once on a trip to Las Vegas, so he had some knowledge of King Tut. He had visited the mock burial chamber in the museum and had seen the treasures as they would have looked when Howard Carter, the English archaeologist, discovered the tomb in 1922. He flicked through the pages: "The white crown of the King of Upper Egypt was placed inside the red crown of the King of Lower Egypt..."

He turned another page and his eyes rested on the sacred cat mummy, *Bast.* Egyptians were cool to honor cats as sacred, he thought, turning the page again. Brrrrr! a shudder ran up his spine. There was a black and white photograph of a dried corpse, arms crossed on the chest and its face almost perfectly intact, but leathery looking.

"I despise mummies and zombies," he muttered. "They give me the creeps!" It was just the initial shock of looking at something so long dead and dehydrated, yet in a way he was fascinated by how the embalmed skin had survived for over five-thousand years, and this had been an actual person with real feelings like his own.

Mrs. Nicholas began to speak again and this time Calder listened.

"Your homework assignment is to research information about the gods of Egypt. Not the Pharaohs, but the gods!"

she directed. "If anyone has an artifact, feel free to share with the rest of the class." Calder thought of bringing the *shabti*, the *scarab*, and *Bast*, then immediately dismissed the idea.

"Okay put your chairs away and leave your desks tidy, please," said Mrs. Nicholas. She was fairly relaxed and Calder thought she had an exotic face like Queen Nefertiti. She encouraged open discussion and many students stayed behind to chat with her about the lesson or an experience they might have had, which may or may not relate to the day's lessons. Regardless, Calder gathered up his books into his orange and gray backpack and slid quietly out of the classroom.

At the gate, Cody Kenyon and two other thugs were waiting for him. Calder thought about turning back towards campus, but decided it might make him look cowardly, so he braced himself for the onslaught. He strode towards them with a determined look on his face, but with a sick feeling in his gut. As Calder tried to pass, Cody stood aside and let his brutish buddy grab Calder by the backpack, slamming him mercilessly into the chain-link fence. Cody wasn't going to risk a detention, so he got his cohorts to do his dirty work this time.

"Cat got your tongue, Greaseball?" he snorted, bringing his face eye to eye with Calder's. Dude, you have foul breath and ferocious, quivering eyes, thought Calder, but he remained silent, his scalp pressed fiercely into the metal fence. He studied his adversary's face at close range, noting each fiery red eyelash, made redder by the angry porcine blue eyes. He scrutinized each golden hair of Cody's contorted unibrow and each blocked pore surrounding his piggish snout. One minor quake and they might erupt like Mount Vesuvius. Calder wanted to close his eyes, but he was transfixed. They were already off campus, so he was tempted to kick him in the groin and run, but he knew that against three bullies he didn't have much of a chance. So, he just grabbed his assailant's arm and pushed him aside, straightened up his ruffled tee-shirt, and rubbed his tortured head. This time they let him pass.

"Next time you're minced meat, Hippy Boy," snarled Kenyon.

"Get a life, Man!" blurted Calder. "You are a sad human being, as insignificant as a pimple on my butt cheek. Just an annoyance, nothing more!" Cody stopped in shock, puzzled over Calder's words. The other bullies cracked up laughing as Cody realized he just *Got Served*, Big Time!

Calder caught up to Derick in the canyon. It was a hot day and they hadn't ridden their bikes. He told Derick all about his close encounter. Derick *high-fived* him and said, "Awesome, Dude! Words *are* mightier than the fist." He couldn't believe Calder had stood up to three thugs. As they trod the familiar path home, they laughed hysterically at his audacity, and his reference to his butt cheek.

"Mom, did you know that the Latin name for a duck-billed platypus is Ornithorhyncus Paradoxis?" Calder asked nonchalantly as he entered his house. "And can we please have cheese enchiladas for dinner?" His mom was in the kitchen, but she wasn't preparing enchiladas. He never mentioned his scuffle with Cody Kenyon. He rarely did!

"Ornitho what?" answered Jenna. "How was school?"

"Oh, alright," Calder dodged the question as he dropped his backpack on the kitchen floor, grabbed a banana from the fruit bowl, and headed outside to feed to his two iguanas. Dinner turned out to be one of Calder's other favorites: chicken and apple sausage (brown and juicy) -- carrots (raw and crisp, the way he liked them) -- bowtie noodles (with lashings of butter and just a sprinkle of black pepper) -- and the promise of enchiladas tomorrow.

After supper, Calder surfed the web for some Egyptian god *info*, downloading several interesting files on the gods' names in the time of Aten. He found a time-line chart for the reign of Amenhotep III to the end of the reign of Horemheb -- the era during which Tutankhamen was born, inherited the throne, and died at the young age of nineteen.

"Wow, Tut was just a kid," Calder mumbled as he printed it out. He found another site that listed the animals and gods of ancient Egypt. He liked this site because the hieroglyphs looked like *Wingdings*, a code font on his word processor: ○☜☒◆□♒☇☜   He printed it, then read on and found that Ibis was listed thus: "Regarded as re-incarnation of Thoth, the ibis was sacred to the god of knowledge, who had the form of an ibis-headed man."

Calder wondered for a while about reincarnation. Could his soul have been reincarnated from *Calder, the Knight-in-training?* Perhaps we have some new lessons to learn in each consecutive life! thought Calder. If this were the case, what lesson had he learned from his previous existence that he felt was useful in the new millennium? Responsibility -- caring for his pet, Jack, just as now he took care of his iguanas, his cat, his fish, and his finches. Every villager in medieval times knew what was expected of them; everyone had something to contribute for the benefit of all. Family, team spirit, and community spirit, were one and the same. They were important then, just as they are today, he thought. Kids didn't have computers, televisions, or video games, but what they never had they never missed, decided Calder. And in real life, just as in *virtual reality*, the object was to advance, to overcome obstacles, and above all, to survive.

Life in medieval England was pretty similar to present day, except for school, medicine, and technology. Kids back then learned all they needed to know at home, or during an apprenticeship. They played, did chores, danced, sang, played instruments, slept in beds, sat around the hearth, dodged the rain, and occasionally fought each other in a joust. He wished he could challenge Cody Kenyon to a round in the jousting arena. Then it would be fair, one on one.

We did play a sport that was a lot like soccer, Calder chuckled, as he remembered the pig bladder plopping around all over Kirkfield. He was happy that he hadn't been the one to put his lips to the bladder to inflate it! Yeukk!

Calder missed Thornhill. He took another look at his Norman helmet sitting on top of its home-made wooden stand. His mom had searched for a hat stand for the helmet, but when she saw that the only ones available were either expensive canvas millinery stands or cheap *Styrofoam* wig stands, she had told Calder that he could figure out a better way, by making use of the discarded scraps of wood his dad left lying around in the garage.

Calder remembered how resourceful his medieval friends had been too. If they needed something that wasn't readily available, they would have to make it themselves. So, he had made his own helmet stand. He used a 12 x 12 inch flat board for the base and a tall 4"x4" piece of lumber for the upright stand, screwed in from the bottom.

It was the perfect height to show off his Norman helmet, since the chain mail hung down the back and cascaded perfectly onto the wooden shelf above the computer, right next to the Viking poster he had brought back from the Jorvik Viking Museum in York.

Using the Norman helmet, would Calder be able to teleport back to medieval Thornhill from the comfort of his own bedroom? He stared fixedly at the reflections in the hand-beaten metal and vowed to try as soon as day turned to night.

Let the Joust Begin

The helmet beckoned him, but he had several more chores to do before he would be able to attempt the trip back to 1470. First, Calder slipped the roster of Egyptian god names and the timeline into his backpack, glanced over the list of spelling words for Friday's test, then completed six math problems. He hastily pushed the math paper back into his math file and went to clean his teeth. Then he pulled on his pajama bottoms and decided to wear his oversized long-sleeved thermal tee-shirt, which reminded him of his medieval leggings and woolen tunic. Now he was ready to visit medieval Thornhill.

About ten minutes went by before his mom popped her head into his room and saw that Calder was reading. She smiled and said, "Goodnight Calder." He had known that she would look in on him, and now it would be safe to go. "G'night! he replied.

When Jenna had returned to the living room, Calder

slipped out of bed. Carefully taking the helmet down from its stand, he placed it on his head. Since it was quite heavy and about three sizes too big, the nose guard came way down beyond his freckly nose. He sat in his black leather swivel chair and closed his eyes, thinking of his medieval friends, Abigail, Thomas, and Hugo. After a while he opened his eyes wide, half expecting to be with them, but he was still in his room in the twenty-first century.

Fifteen minutes later, his mom poked her head around the door. Calder was asleep in the chair wearing the heavy helmet. He had fallen sideways and was resting on the arm of the chair. She took off his helmet, gently untangling his long hair from the chain mail, then returned the helmet to the stand and attempted to guide him, in a sort of sleepwalking manner, back into bed. Jenna covered him with his soft down duvet and closed the door.

On the other side of the centuries, Calder found himself in Whitby, on the east coast of Yorkshire. The place where he had bought the helmet. This is the wrong place and perhaps even the wrong time, he feared, as he looked around at the abbey. He saw that it was quite pristine, not a ruin as he had seen it with his nana. Calder soon realized that he *was* in the right era, but Whitby was so-o-o far from Thornhill. It was at this moment that the memories of the twenty-first century faded into a mist.

"Ovver 'ere, Lad," shouted a middle-aged man.

"Heigh-ho!" yelled Calder as he ran to greet his uncle. "I was looking at the abbey up on yonder cliff."

"Aye, Lad," replied Uncle Eldred. "Tis a beauty, but we've got business t' take care of afore this day is out. We have my woven cloth t' sell 'ere, then on t' York, and kippers t' take back t' Thornhill." Calder looked back at the abbey standing alone on the cliffs, whipped by the howling winds of the North Sea. The little fishing town of Whitby hugged the estuary below, where there was a hustle and bustle in the harbor; people were selling their *catch of the day*. "Cockles, mussels, 'errings, cod! Freshly caught this morn," shouted one fisherman's wife.

Calder and Eldred walked down the endless stone steps to the cobbled streets below. On *Henrietta Street* was a smoke-blackened cottage with a slate roof. Calder peered inside. Dozens of rust-colored filleted fish dangled in the smoke, on lengths of twine strung across the room like socks on a washing line.

"Tis like a colony of wrinkly weathered bats in a dank and smoky cave," he gasped.

"Aye, smoking 'errings turns 'em into kippers," his uncle explained.

"And makes 'em so-o much tastier than bats!" laughed Calder.

Eldred showed his fine woolen fabric to the kipper vendor and they agreed upon a trade, twenty-four kippers for a soft green woolen blanket. The vendor wrapped up the kippers in a small brown paper parcel, then Calder and Eldred headed back to where their horse was waiting. He was a large, shiny black horse with a white blaze on his forehead and shaggy white hair covering his hooves. The horse's name was Ned.

"Sit thee down and rest a while!" said Eldred as he opened the carefully wrapped package of kippers.

"Mmmmm, delicious!" beamed Calder, devouring a piece of smoked brown fish. He licked his fishy fingers and wrapped up the remaining kippers for later.

Eldred sold the rest of his cloth and fine cloaks to a Dutch tradesman who owned a boat in the harbor. As Eldred and the tradesman bartered back and forth, trying to agree upon a price, Calder watched and learned how to negotiate. He busied himself unloading Eldred's merchandise, but paid close attention to how business was being conducted. Finally, he saw the tradesman count out eight silver coins and place them in a leather pouch, which he then handed to Eldred.

"Now we must make haste t' be in York afore dark," announced Eldred. "On the morrow we shall purchase dyes for my fabrics, and from Portugal, we'll buy olive oil, salt, figs, and wine for the family."

"Portugal," Calder repeated excitedly, wondering what that faraway country might be like.

The journey from Whitby to York was treacherous. Ned made it to the crest of the first steep hill before the wind turned cold. Eldred allowed him to pause and drink from a freshwater stream, which sprang from the rocks and ran in a gorge down the edge of the dirt road. Calder cupped his hands and drank too. Now the barren purple moor stretched out before them like a legendary sleeping dragon. It was going to be a long, lonely journey. There were no trees on the moor, and the wind howled like a wild dog as it swept across the *Hole of Horcumb*.

"What be that wailing sound?" asked Calder, as he covered his head and shoulders with his hood and wrapped the warm red cloak round himself.

"Tis the wutherin', Lad," answered Uncle Eldred.

"Wutherin'?" questioned Calder.

"Aye, wutherin'!" Eldred explained. "The sound the wind makes as it crosses the empty moor, like air blowing across the top of an empty bottle."

With the steepest hill behind them, Ned was able to pick up the pace and gallop along at a fair speed. Calder rode behind his uncle and clung on for dear life as the wind whipped like a cat-o'-nine-tails at his face.

Less than two hours later, they were entering the walled city of York, the biggest city Calder had ever seen. They paid a toll of one farthing to cross the bridge into the city. Built right onto the bridge (over the Foss) was a cobbler's shop, a fletcher's shop (selling arrows and quivers), and a cloth merchant's shop. Multi-colored banners hung from the city wall and flapped in the wind. "Aye verily, a most spectacular sight!" glowed a wide-eyed Calder as they passed through the archway of Monk Bar.

There was much merriment that evening. Eldred and Calder went into the tavern for a cup of hot cider and to warm themselves by the fire. They ordered spit-roasted chicken and potatoes, and they chatted to the local merchants. Because of the rules of the *York Guild*, Eldred wouldn't be allowed to sell any of his wares in York. Only York merchants could sell in York, but Calder didn't care; he was enthralled. A minstrel played the lute and a jester juggled and performed magic. He would have stayed up all night, but Eldred was tired, so they paid a penny for a comfortable room and Ned was taken to the stables to rest, cool off, and be brushed down.

After a breakfast of bacon and eggs, Calder and Eldred shopped for the dyes and Portuguese oils, salt, figs, and wine. Calder had never seen such exotic goods; the smells of imported cheeses and meats tantalized his nostrils.

After stowing their purchases in the leather saddle bags, Eldred secured his pouch of coins to his belt and pulled his cloak around himself, in case they were set upon by thieves like the infamous Robyn of Loxley, who had been an outlaw a century earlier. *Robyn* had been known to steal from the rich to give to the poor. After their trading, they might be seen to be wealthier than they actually were. According to Eldred, "Some notorious highwaymen were known to steal the copper pennies off the eyes of a dead man!"

"Why doth a dead man have pennies on his eyes?" Calder asked, full of curiosity.

"Why, t' keep 'is eyelids closed, o' course," answered Eldred, snapping the reins.

They galloped hard and fast through some of the greenest countryside in England, over the Vale of York, in the direction of Sandal Castle. Eldred was an expert horseman like Calder's father, William. He ducked under branches and leaped over streams, taking shortcuts across the meadows. Calder enjoyed the gallop and learned from Eldred when to duck or swerve, and when to hang on for dear life.

The weather had settled and was even almost balmy by the time they reached Sandal Castle. Jordan was a knight there, and as Calder thought himself a knight-in-training, he needed some expert advice.

"Methinks I need to learn how to joust and how to fight. Wilt thou show me, Brother?" pleaded Calder eagerly, as Eldred went off to water the horse and to buy a couple of pheasants for dinner.

Sir Jordan showed Calder the portcullis gate, the drawbridge, and the battering ram used to beat down other castle doors, but Calder's favorite instrument of war was a siege machine or *trebuchet*.

"It doth look like a great sling-shot on wheels!" Calder exclaimed.

"Tis exactly so," confirmed his brother. Sir Jordan was more than six feet tall, with long dark brown hair, a short goatee beard, and dark bushy eyebrows above his clear hazel eyes. He made quite a handsome knight and Calder was proud of him. Sir Jordan slipped his leather gloves onto Calder's hands and covered them with metal gauntlets, then he took off his helmet and placed it firmly on Calder's head. Calder could feel the weight of the armor and he found it hard to move, let alone climb onto a horse. However, he wanted to impress Sir Jordan, so he planned to do his very best.

"Wilt thou teach me how to joust, Brother?" pleaded Calder.

"Aye, if it be jousting that thou liketh, come hither and I will show thee where the knights of Sandal do practice afore a tournament," proclaimed Sir Jordan as he led Calder towards the jousting arena. He showed him the *quintain*, which was used as a swiveling target, and helped Calder onto the horse, offering him a long wooden lance. Calder couched the long handgrip under his right arm, but struggled to balance the shaft horizontally in front of himself.

"Make sure thy visor is securely down, in order to protect thy face from splinters. Then ride thee towards the quintain and aim to strike the shield in the center," directed Sir Jordan. "Sit thee tall and keep thy focus." Calder looked at the quintain. A shield was mounted on his side of the "T" and the crossbar swiveled on a central spike at the top of a tall wooden pole. On the other end of the crossbar was a swinging bag of sand, used as a weight to take the force of the blow. It could also deliver a good *wallop* to the jousting knight, if he didn't get out of the way when it swung around in a circle.

Calder shifted his weight in the saddle, trying to control his fear and excitement, which were now gripping and flipping his stomach into knots. His lack of full protective armor made him feel a little vulnerable, but he did have the lance, a small convex shield known as an ecranche, and the enormous helmet. Sir Jordan led the horse at a gentle trot in the direction of the quintain. In Calder's mind, he was a gallant knight in a royal tournament, speeding thunderously towards his opponent. He raised the lance and aimed for his target. At the moment the coronel impacted the shield, he felt a jolt in his shoulder socket. The quintain spun on its axis as the end of Calder's lance glanced off the target and flew in an arc above Sir Jordan's head. At the same time, Calder ducked to let the sandbag spin, with a *WHOOSHing* sound, over his helmet. Fortunately, no-one was hurt!

Calder was ecstatic as he eagerly tried to dismount. This had been his first lesson in becoming a chivalrous knight of Sandal Castle! Jordan ceremoniously stood his sword upright in front of Calder, with the tip resting on a large tussock of grass and the hilt at Calder's chest.

"Mark my word, Brother, thou wilt be a mighty knight. Already thou knowest how to ride a steed and how to fight with swords. Practice thy jousting in Kirkfield with Hugo. Thou couldst ride Ned and use a long pole as thy lance, but take heed not to kill thyself, nor to injure each other. Because verily, our dear mother would not like that," advised Sir Jordan.

"Nay, she would not like that!" laughed Calder. "But I

will soon be ready to joust with thee, Sir Jordan." The young wannabe knight imagined himself charging, with the lance aimed at knocking his brother off his horse.

He had enjoyed his time with Sir Jordan, but as dusk was upon them, he and Eldred were back on the road towards Thornhill. They galloped fast through Horbury. From there, they could make out the distant fire beacon, glowing like a setting sun into the silhouette of the dark plateau. They were only a mile from home, yet Calder, overcome with fatigue, dozed on the horse behind his uncle and dreamed of a tournament in front of the King of England.

His arms were wrapped around his uncle's waist, grasping tightly onto Eldred's belt. To make sure he didn't slide off the horse, Eldred reached behind and held on to Calder with one hand, while clutching the reins with the other, as they raced towards home.

Double Take

Calder woke up groggily and found himself back in his California bedroom. His mother knocked on his door. "C'mon Calder, time to get ready for school. You'll be late."

Calder rubbed his eyes. Was it just a dream? Am I really a knight-in-training? He closed his eyes again and rolled over onto something crumpled beneath his ribs. Raising his chest, he slipped his right hand under himself and grabbed the soft crumpled object. How did this get into my bed? he thought, pulling the large leather glove onto his hand.

"Oh no, it's Jordan's gauntlet!" he gasped and removed it quickly. "But this proves I was in medieval England. There's no doubt about that now!" Calder remembered that he'd been riding towards Thornhill, clinging to his uncle's back, when he must have fallen asleep. He'd hoped to see Abigail, Hugo, and Thomas again, but on that trip he hadn't been able to reunite with them.

No time to go back there right now, he thought. I'd be late for school. So he jumped out of bed and pushed the gauntlet into the front pouch of his backpack with the Egyptian artifacts. Thinking back to the moment before he found the glove, he felt sure he'd heard a *Bang-Bang-Bang*, like a fist on the side wall. Eerily familiar, he frowned as he pulled on his surfer tee. He remembered a high profile California court case: *If the glove doesn't fit, you must acquit.* "Hmm -- and if the glove fits, you must have zits," Calder snickered. The silly saying rattled around in his head. Now that he was faced with his own glove evidence, it seemed to fill him with ironic intrigue!

The telephone rang and Derick's voice came down the line, "I'm riding to school today if you want to meet me at the corner."

"I'll be ready in five..." answered Calder.

"Okay, see ya," they agreed. Calder took a bite of his toast, a swig of orange juice, and chomped down a multivitamin. He fastened his bicycle helmet, opened the garage door, and sped down the street like a medieval knight on his tournament charger.

Azule had been inundated with submissions for the sixth grade magazine. After school, the girls decided to get together at Ellie's house so that they could sort out the great from the mediocre. Ellie's mom provided oatmeal cookies and hot chocolate made with soy milk. Since Azule had arrived early, she and Ellie were sorting out the pile of submissions when Maddy, Sarah, and Jade arrived. Ellie invited them into her spacious bedroom and spread the papers on the coral-colored, plush carpet. Ellie organized three piles: *Definite, Maybe,* and *No Way.*

There was a short essay on gray whales, another about the local tide pools, and one more about skateboarding, typical stories written by kids who live on the California coast. Joe had submitted his *Tubular Surf* story, which Azule thought was quite impressive, so she put it on the *Definite* pile.

"It's great to see him write," she said enthusiastically. "He usually just plays football." This had brought out another hidden talent in Joe, because he was equally passionate about surfing.

Since the Solar Flare was now open to all grades, Maddy picked up a poem submitted by a fourth-grader. It was entitled *Winter*, and she read:

> Isn't snow a lovely sight,
> Crisp, and deep, and white?
> It sparkles as I walk along
> And makes me want to sing a song.
> Snow is cold
> And turns to ice,
> But I think that
> It's rather nice.

Azule placed it on the *Maybe* pile. "You might want to switch that to the *Definite* pile," suggested Ellie. "We didn't receive any other poetry entries." Azule slid it onto the *Definite* pile; after all you didn't hear much about snow in Southern California, and it was simple but charming.

Azule mentioned Calder's drawing, but Sarah objected. "He's too weird. Why would we want that Bozo's drawings in our magazine?"

As usual, Azule came to Calder's defense. "Don't call

him weird, Sarah. He's actually pretty cool -- most of the time. He's my friend and his drawings are great."

"Anyway, we said we'd consider everyone's effort without prejudice," added Ellie.

"It's everyone's magazine, not ours exclusively," continued Jade.

Sarah shrugged, realizing she was outnumbered. "Well, okay," she reluctantly agreed.

Maddy suggested the centerfold: "The middle pages for the Middle Ages," she quipped. "We could give him half a page for his drawing, and hopefully, if he came through with an accompanying story, that could take up the other half and maybe even spread onto the next page."

"Done!" said Azule. "Joe's surf composition can fill up the other three-quarters of a page."

"Perfect," agreed Maddy, "but we'll have to reduce Calder's sketch on the copying machine to make it fit the page." They were planning two full sheets of white paper, stapled in the middle to form eight pages in all. They planned to keep it monochromatic, according to Azule.

"Ooooh, that's a big word, did someone swallow a dictionary today?" asked Jade sarcastically.

"It literally means one color. So, black ink on white paper," explained Azule.

"May I design the cover page?" Ellie asked. "I'm visualizing palm trees, surf, and shells surrounded by a hibiscus border."

"Sounds great!" they all agreed.

"Don't forget some radiating sun rays," suggested Maddy. "After all, it is *The Sixth Grade Solar Flare*."

"Then we should do flares, not rays," argued Ellie.

"Hmm, you have a point," admitted Maddy, "but let's not

get picky, picky, picky!"

The meeting adjourned and the girls headed down for their snacks in the dining room. Azule volunteered to talk to Calder at recess the following day. Ellie vowed to find a crossword puzzle designer.

"I have a humongous book of riddles and puzzles if you can't find anyone," offered Jade.

Things were coming together quickly. The *No Way* pile at first outweighed the *Definite*, but not wanting to discourage people from submitting, most *Maybes* were shuffled across to the *Definite* pile and quite a few rejects became *Maybes*.

"The *Maybes* that aren't used this month could be reconsidered next time," suggested Ellie.

"By the end of the second week it will all be sorted out," sighed Azule, dunking her cookie into the chocolate soy. "Out of chaos..." she began, then popping the cookie into her mouth, she never completed the sentence.

Azule approached Calder at recess. He was sitting with Derick and Joe. They were examining something that looked like a gardener's leather glove, only longer and more flared at the wrist.

"May I take your sketch and make a copy of it, Calder?" she asked politely. "I'll get it back to you by the end of lunch recess -- and Joe, your story was accepted too. It's awesome!" Joe grinned as Calder nonchalantly reached inside his backpack, pulled out the sketchpad, and handed it to her. Azule asked Derick if he would like to be the weather man, under the pseudonym: *Meteorologist Mike*.

"I like it already," he decided. She explained that his job would be to chart an average temperature and the rainfall for each month. "B-but it's always around seventy-five degrees at the coast, and there's little or no rainfall -- which would be so boring," he complained.

"Okay, have fun with it then," suggested Azule. "Throw a little scientific drama into the recipe."

"That's more my style!" he agreed, bobbing his head slowly and suddenly feeling very *Cool*.

Azule was slightly intrigued by the glove that Calder was holding, but thought it was of little consequence until Joe blurted out, "Calder has a knight's gauntlet from the Middle Ages." Azule thought it certainly looked as though it was from another era, but it was in near perfect condition.

"So how could it have survived the centuries so well?" was Azule's immediate reaction.

"Well, Calder brought it..."

"Don't!" exploded Calder, halting Joe in mid-sentence.

"It belonged to Calder's knight," Joe finished regardless.

Azule leaned forward and questioned Joe further, "How did it get here -- by Hawk-Post?"

Nobody thought Azule's quip was very funny; there was a unanimous groan of disapproval before Joe countered, "No, it came by Chain-Mail, of course!" Azule smiled wryly at his quick wit, but nevertheless, there was something magnetizing about the glove, and she wanted to know more about how Calder had come to own it.

"Write about it for the magazine, then!" was her only retort. "I want to know everything. We'll print your story alongside your sketch." Azule wouldn't miss an opportunity to entice a good story out of Calder. She knew he was capable; he'd already shared some of his adventures with her. "We still have ten days before the deadline," she said. "I'll reserve half a page for you, or even a page and a half, if you can manage it." Calder just smiled his pencil-thin smile and sighed. He stuffed the gauntlet into his backpack and set off towards the classroom.

It might help me figure it all out if I start to write it down, Calder thought later that evening. He flicked on the computer, pulled up Microsoft Word, and found his notes in the file marked: *Medieval Wanderings*. He had the gauntlet in his hands, but dared not pull it onto his hand yet, in case he was whisked away across the centuries. He needed time to sort out this entire bizarre adventure before his next trip, but he knew he must get the gauntlet back to Sir Jordan before too long.

He wondered about what happened to Medieval Calder, after *he* returned to the present. Did he just disappear, or did he go on living his life regardless of Millennium Calder? Uncle Eldred hadn't been surprised to see him in Whitby, so he presumed that Medieval Calder had traveled there with him from Thornhill. "Hmmmm, curiouser and curiouser," muttered Calder. He swiveled his chair to face the monitor and started to write: "It first happened about a year ago, on a trip to England. I was in the fields feeding some bad-tempered ponies, when suddenly..."

A couple of weeks later, the *Sixth Grade Solar Flare* was hot off the press. Sarah and Jade were in charge of promotion and distribution. Their first issue coincided with the sale of Girl Scout cookies. Parents and students alike were snatching up the magazines, and the donations were accumulating in a stone jar. Sarah loved the sound of coins clinking into the jar.

"Music to my ears," she dramatized. "We'll be able to afford manicures and pedicures at this rate."

"So much for camping out!" giggled Jade.

"Creature comforts are what it's all about," continued Sarah. "Don't forget, I'm a *Lady of Leisure!*" The other girls laughed, they knew she was joking, although they also knew that she certainly would never refuse a modicum of pampering.

Ellie had done a wonderful job designing the front page. *Sixth Grade Solar Flare* was written in a rainbow arch across the top of the page. Two palms swayed up the left side and the fronds filled the space in the top left corner. Below the lettering, rolled a tube-shaped wave, and in the bottom right corner was an assortment of seashells: nautilus, conches, and cowries. All this was tied together by a floral border, a lei of hibiscus and plumeria flowers.

"Effective design!" commented one parent as she read the captions on the cover page: *Premier Issue. Edited and Printed by Participating Sixth-grade Students.* She was very impressed. There was a list of featured articles, a photograph of the surfing brothers, Joe and Dave Vedder, and the introduction to Joe's surf story, ...*to be continued on page five.* Meteorologist Mike predicted: "Great quantities of sun with intermittent golf-ball-sized hail, warty toad showers, and the possibility of a mile wide water spout on the Pacific Ocean." He plotted his predictions based on last month's weather. Cardiff-by-the-Sea had been overcast all month, like an early June Gloom. "We'll have no more of that!" he wrote. "Nothing but blue skies and green lights from now on!" It was a bit of a zany concoction, but Azule loved it.

Calder didn't want to see his own illustrated story in print. He felt vulnerable and was wishing he'd never submitted it, but then several students came up to him and threw some very positive comments his way. A few *high-fives* later, he was beginning to feel the ground beneath his feet. In fact, he didn't know how he was going to react to this new wave of attention. His drawing was printed on page four. The story covered the other half of the page and almost three-quarters of page five. His story was so credible, and at the same time, so incredible, that many of his peers started to see Calder in a different light. No longer was he known as the *Wild Hippy Boy*, he was now the *Millennium Knight*. Azule was happy to have had a part in it; she really was his guardian.

A week earlier, when Calder had finished writing the essay at his computer desk, he had been exhausted! It had been cathartic, but his mind was still racing. As his thoughts traveled back to Thornhill, he'd started to make comparisons between then and now. He felt that there were fewer pressures on a boy his age in the fifteenth century, but childhood was definitely shorter. He thought about his friends back there: Hugo, Thomas, and Abigail. Thomas was already an apprentice cobbler at age eleven, and Hugo was planning to ask Mr. Bradford if he would take him on as an apprentice blacksmith. Abigail would more than likely be a home-maker, as all the women of medieval times were, but she also had a penchant for writing. With her Aunt Jenna's help, she would at least learn to write out the parchment registers for the church, noting all births, deaths, and marriages, etc. Generally, only the most privileged women learned to write in those days, but because Gwenna and Abigail were both descended from Sir John de Thornhill, the privilege was theirs. Finally, there was, of course, Medieval Calder, who was destined to become a knight at Sandal Castle alongside his brother,

Sir Jordan. Millennium Calder's dream of knighthood was being fulfilled, even if it were in a parallel reality.

Calder hadn't been able to see his friends on his last trip to medieval England as he'd fallen asleep before he and Eldred arrived at Thornhill. The next morning Calder had woken up in his California bed. The more Calder thought about all of his friends, the more he realized how much alike Joe and Hugo were. For that matter, Derick and Thomas were similar too.

"Wow!" he muttered as though in a hypnotic dream. "And Azule *is* Abigail!" He must go back to see them! Besides, Sir Jordan would be searching for his glove.

Calder stuffed his homework and the essay into his file and zipped it into his backpack. He sat back in the chair with his woolen blanket around him and pulled the glove onto his right hand. He definitely didn't want to wear the helmet because it might take him back to Whitby, and although he enjoyed it there, it was too far away from Thornhill. By wearing the gauntlet, Calder hoped he would arrive back at Sandal Castle with Jordan, or even better, slip quietly into the village of Thornhill.

As he sat with his eyes closed, Calder felt sure he could smell the morning bread baking in his medieval home.

May Day! May Day!

Calder awoke on his horse-hair mattress, his head nestled on his soft eiderdown pillow.

"Yes, I made it!" he exclaimed, stretching his arms above his head and yawning. "Totally awesome, I'm back in Thornhill."

Moments later, he couldn't remember why he'd felt so ecstatic. Methinks, I must have had a fine dream, or perhaps I am happy to be home in mine own bed after traveling so far. He could smell the bread and bacon cooking for breakfast. As he opened the curtain of his four-poster bed, he saw his mother, Gwenna, pulling a freshly baked loaf from the stone oven next to the fireplace.

"Hugo came by early this morn, but thou wert so tired from thy journey that I did not like to waken thee, my son," explained Gwenna.

"Oh many thanks, Mother, I did have a wonderful sleep this morn."

"Hugo sayeth to tell thee that they would be laiking in Kirkfield." Calder immediately knew what the message meant; they were playing in the field next to the church. He straightened his bed and saw the leather gauntlet on the floor. Alas, he thought, this gauntlet belongeth to Jordan. I must return it post-haste. He pulled his tunic over his long-sleeved woolen top and leggings, and ran his fingers through his tousled hair.

"Come prithee, sit thee down and eat first, Calder," willed Gwenna. On the table she placed a wooden bread board with a chunk of crusty bread and a carving knife. In front of Calder she placed a platter of hot crispy bacon and fried eggs, and a mug of fresh goat's milk. Calder was ravenous; he hadn't eaten dinner the previous night because he'd fallen asleep on his journey home. He ate and drank as though he hadn't been fed for a week. Gwenna kissed him on the forehead and brushed back his wild blond hair.

"Forget not thy creatures," she reminded him. "I did feed the hens and goats, but I was unable to feed thy kestrel. He also needeth exercise as thou wert gone for several days!"

"I will not forget, Mother," Calder reassured her, "but Jack probably found a rodent or two to eat in the outer house." He wrapped his long leather belt around his hips and pushed the wooden sword into it, but it felt like a child's toy, so he immediately discarded it. He picked up the gauntlet and laid it on his bed. "Might I ride to Sandal to return the gauntlet to Jordan?"

"Ask thine uncle if thou may'st borrow the horse, but I would be happier if thou wouldst ride there with a goodfellow," answered Gwenna.

"Tis but four miles, Ma'am, but as it is thy wish, I will ask

Hugo or Thomas if they might accompany me," he replied.

On the way to Kirkfield, Calder stopped at Eldred's house. He was busy trying out the new dyes and had made a beautiful Lincoln green; it was the color of oak leaves.

"A person might hide well in the forest, wearing a tunic of such a natural hue!" exclaimed Calder.

"Aye, like Robyn the Hudde of Loxley?" answered Eldred. "How wouldst thou like a tunic in this shade of green?"

"Methinks I might like that very much indeed, Uncle."

"Then this length of fabric shall be payment for the help thou gavest me on the trip to Whitby and York," Eldred said, as he measured off a couple of arm-lengths of fabric. "Perhaps thy mother will sew for thee a new tunic."

"Oh, many thanks Uncle, but I have one more favor to ask of thee. Might I borrow Ned this day?"

"Aye, but whither would'st thou be riding so soon after such a long trip?" Eldred inquired. Calder explained about the glove and Eldred agreed to let him borrow the horse. He helped Calder onto Ned and handed him the reins, reminding him to go easy with the horse as it was supposed to be his resting day, after the long journey to Whitby.

Calder rode proudly up the street towards a commotion. Robert Ludwell had been caught stealing a pig from the farmer's field and he was in the stocks for a few days of public humiliation. As it was a nether stock, only his feet were locked into the rack, while Ludwell sat on the attached bench, wailing like a baby as the villagers pelted him with rotten tomatoes and eggs. Calder found it such a humiliating punishment, but he was in high spirits, so he kicked gently at Ned's sides and the horse took off at a slow trot. Since he couldn't go through the churchyard with the horse, Calder circled the village again and trotted down the *ginnel* that led to Kirkfield.

"Calder ist here, Calder ist here!" shouted Thomas as he ran to greet them. Calder helped his friend onto the horse, as Hugo sprang up from behind the wall and pelted them with dry cow pats.

"We missed thee," Hugo shouted. "How was thy journey?" Calder steadied Ned parallel to the wall and from there, Hugo hurled himself onto the horse behind his two friends. They had no saddle, just one of Eldred's soft woven blankets tied beneath Ned's belly with a girth strap. "Three knights on a fine charger!" yelled Hugo as the horse cantered easily around the field.

With great excitement Calder narrated his adventures in the city of York and the town of Whitby. He told them about the abbey on the cliffs and the kipper cottage. He described the moor and the incredible walled city with its majestic Cathedral. Hugo and Thomas listened attentively.

"I have barely ventured out of Thornhill, yet thou hast seen the North Sea, fishing towns, and great walled cities," praised Thomas, who lived in a tiny stone cottage near the market cross. He was an apprentice cobbler to his father. He helped cut out the shapes of leather with shears, he trimmed them with a trinket knife, and when his father had shaped and stitched the shoes on the iron last, it was Thomas' job to make the holes for the laces by using a round, pointed tool called an awl. He also waxed the ends of the leather laces and threaded them to tie at the ankle. Thomas' father was working on a new fastening device, a little wooden toggle fastened with a loop of leather.

"Oh, how I would like such a pair of new boots for the winter to wear with my Lincoln green tunic," gushed Calder.

"I shall place thee an order right away, and fashion

them myself," laughed Thomas.

"Aye, but canst thou come with us this day to Sandal Castle?"

"Alas, we must ask our parents," said Hugo.

"First let us go into the kirk," suggested Calder. "We have much time and the weather is fine." At the church the three wannabe knights dismounted, Calder tethered Ned to the iron post outside the Lych-gate, and they entered the church.

"Tis so-o-o dark in here," whispered Thomas.

"I see nothing!" added Hugo.

"Relax and let thine eyes grow accustomed to the light," advised Calder.

It was very quiet. All that was to be heard was the high melodic twittering of a skylark outside and three boys breathing. The spring sunlight shone in through a fine medieval stained-glass window at the east end of the church, lighting the whole chapel in a spectrum of vibrant colors.

Calder walked towards the light. The colors streaked onto a stone effigy of a cross-legged knight, low to the flagstone floor. The knight's helmeted head lay upon a stone pillow. His stone sword ran from his praying gloved hands to his pointed-toe boots (just as Calder had held the sword the previous day with Sir Jordan). Under the knight's stone boots was a sleek stone dog. It was the oldest monument in the Savile Chapel and it was dedicated to Calder's great, great, great-grandfather, Sir John, first knight of Thornhill. Running his hands over the smooth, cold stone helmet, Calder vowed to become a knight like Sir John and Sir Jordan, in the tradition of his family.

The other boys were looking at a monument, which

looked like a four poster bed with three figures carved upon it: Lord John Savile the Elder and his two wives. Their hands were carved in oak at their chests, pointing in prayer towards their chins. Derick was trying to decipher the inscription as Calder traced the carved lettering with his fingers and read: *"Bonys amonge stonys lys ful steyl, qwylste the sawles wanderes war that God wyl."* He whispered, "Bones among stones lie very still, while the souls wander wherever God wills."

Sufficiently scared, they all headed for the door, but Calder stopped to look at a tiny gravestone inscribed with a dagger, apparently from the twelfth century. Next to it was the ninth century rune stone dedicated to Osbert, the Anglo-Saxon King killed by the Vikings in York in the year 867 and buried at Thornhill.

Calder paid his respects to his ancestors, then left the church. The other two boys were already outside waiting.

"What took thee so long?" asked Hugo. "We thought the *sawles* had taken thee!"

"Aye, now let us make haste and be off to Sandal," announced Calder. First they rode to Thomas' cottage. It was market day and the crossroads were alive with village vendors. The boys dismounted and Thomas ran in to ask permission. His father said he could play in the market for twenty minutes more, but then he must come back to work as he had many shoes to finish.

"Madame Mortimer hath need of them by t'morrow, lad!" exclaimed the cobbler. Thomas was disappointed. He knew that his childhood days were coming to an end, and he had to be more serious in his endeavors to become a good cobbler like his father. Calder and Hugo were disappointed too, but decided to pass the time with Thomas until he had to resume his work. They tethered Ned close to the stone trough at the base of the market cross and left him there to drink.

Abigail approached the boys after maneuvering herself through the crowd on her newly purchased stilts. "I be taller than everyone in Thornhill," she announced. The boys were happy to see their *Guinevere*. Two plaits from her forehead were braided, like a coronet, around to the back where her raven tresses flowed to her waist. Her sky blue eyes twinkled in the daylight and her tiny linen slippers peeked out from below her velvet dress.

Aunt Catherine joined them and offered each of them a fresh hot-cross bun, which they eagerly accepted. Hugo wanted to attempt to knock a turnip off the wooden stake at the *turnip shy*, so he paid his farthing, stood behind the designated line, and threw the wooden ball as hard as he could. Thud! Down it went on the first throw and Hugo won the turnip.

Thomas was called in to work and Abigail and Catherine continued shopping, so Calder and Hugo rode Ned up the lane, passing food-spattered Ludwell on the bench with his legs outstretched and his feet firmly locked inside the ankle holes. Except for the occasional tomato from a passing villager, the shower of rotting fruits had practically ceased.

"Good morrow!" greeted Calder, hoping to cheer him up, but it wasn't a good day for Ludwell who hung his head in shame.

"Methinks, I should lob mine turnip at him," scoffed Hugo in jest.

Calder stifled his laughter, barely. "Aye, that would cure the knavish *clumperton* of thievery," he giggled.

Hugo's mother was at her weaving loom in a corner of the room, where the sunlight streamed in through the small leaded window. She wore a modest brown dress over her linen blouse, tied at the waist with a leather crossover belt. Her hair was pulled into a scoop at the back of her neck and she wore a little cotton bonnet, tied under her chin. She turned and welcomed the boys, trying to get used to the fact that these youths were no longer children.

"I won a turnip for thee, Mother. May I ride with Calder to see Sir Jordan at Sandal Castle?" Hugo pleaded, all in one breath.

"Many thanks for the turnip, Hugo, but prithee, offer it to Jenna, for I have already prepared one for dinner," she replied. "I trust thou wilt be very careful on thy journey," she cautioned. "Be sure that thou returnest home afore dusk."

It was late morning on a beautiful spring day. Daffodils were growing at the edge of the grass verge, their golden trumpets bobbing freely in the mild breeze. Blossom scented the air and the sky was filled with birdsong. As they trotted towards Calder's cottage, Hugo began to sing: "Morning hath broken, like the first morning..."

Calder joined in: "Blackbird hath spoken, like the first bird..."

At his cottage, Calder dismounted and ran into the outer house. He threw some alfalfa and grain to his goats and hens, and pulled on his gauntlet for the kestrel. The hawk knew the daily procedure; he swiftly flew down onto Calder's outstretched hand.

"Fly thee free for the whole afternoon!" said Calder, releasing Jack and tossing the gauntlet onto the ledge. He entered the house, picked up Jordan's leather glove, and tucked it into his belt.

"We shall return afore dusk!" he called to his mother as she hurried to see them off.

"Fare thee well, and prithee, give my love to Jordan," she said, handing over a chunk of bread with a thick slice of ham for the boys and two carrots for the horse. Calder attached the package to the girth strap. As this was their first journey out of Thornhill without adult supervision, they planned to be very careful.

"Verily, verily, worry not thy pretty head!" replied Calder. Hugo clung to Calder's belt with one hand and grabbed the top of the girth strap with the other. Calder held the reins and tightened his grip on Ned's sides as they galloped down Deadman's Lane and up the other side of the valley towards Horbury, where villagers were preparing for the upcoming May Day festivities.

A maypole stood at the ready in the center of the Green. Each young girl held a garland that radiated out on all sides, making it look like a twenty-foot party hat. The Morris dancers jingled their leg bells as they danced, and a hurdy-gurdy man played a merry tune as the maidens dodged and danced, weaving their multi-colored ribbons around the pole, until the pole at last became a braided masterpiece. The boys watched admiringly as they rode on around the Green and headed towards Sandal.

Jordan was surprised to see Calder and Hugo riding over the drawbridge and into the castle forecourt.

"Did we not meet just yester day?" called Jordan. "And how art thou, Hugo?"

Hugo was pleased to see Jordan as he'd always seemed like a big brother to him too. Calder returned the lost gauntlet and they spent a few minutes showing Hugo around the castle. Before leaving, they led the horse to the water trough, then ate their lunches at the base of the castle ramparts.

On the bridge, Calder shouted over his shoulder, "Our Mother sendeth her love to thee."

"I shall be home to visit in one week," answered Sir Jordan. "Prepare thyselves for a good joust!"

As they had made good time, Calder suggested they ride by way of the new manor. Forgetting Eldred's advice, they galloped furiously around the perimeter of the new moat. The boys were having great fun, ducking and weaving as they rode under oak and sycamore branches, splashing water in all directions, hooting and hollering, and holding on for dear life, but at the last curve Hugo forgot to duck. He was knocked off the horse by a low branch and sent flying backwards, landing hard -- face down -- in the moat!

Calder was devastated to see his friend lying motionless in the water. He dismounted hastily and shouted for help as he ran to pull Hugo from the water. But nobody heard his cries except Jack, who continued circling above the trees. Calder turned Hugo onto his back and cradled his head with his forearm. He checked the side of his throat, but could feel no pulse. Calder was frantic. Hugo was bigger than him and now that his clothes were soaked, he weighed even more. How might I pull this big *clodhopper* out of the moat, he thought, terrified at the possibility of losing his best friend.

Calder looked around, still no help! Time seemed to have gone into slow motion. He looked into Hugo's lifeless eyes.

"Prithee, let this not happen to my goodfellow," he wailed with frustration, then took a breath. "No problems, only solutions!" he reminded himself. Calder took off his own tunic and rolled it under Hugo's head to raise his nose and mouth above the shallow water. He whistled for Ned and the horse came to the edge of the moat. Calder quickly untied the girth strap, made a loop, and secured it around Hugo's ankles, like Ludwell in the stocks. He fastened the other end to the reins. Ned seemed to understand what was going on; he whinnied, but held still until Calder could support Hugo's head and neck.

"Back, boy, back!" ordered Calder as Ned retreated, and together they pulled Hugo clear of the moat. Calder rolled Hugo over onto his belly on the grassy embankment, then placed his arms forward, turned his head to the right, and pushed against his ribs. After a few attempts, a choking gurgle of water gushed from Hugo's mouth, like a gargoyle spewing out rainwater. Hugo uttered a deep groan as Calder pushed again and again. Finally, Hugo spluttered out a ball of frothy green algae.

A muffled "Nay, nay-ay," was all that Hugo could utter, but Calder was glad to hear any sound at all. He removed the girth strap, and with a little encouragement, Hugo pulled his knees under himself and rose shakily to his feet.

"Thou seemest to have survived," sighed Calder with relief, helping Hugo to a nearby tree stump.

"Aaaargh," groaned Hugo, and burped a few more swampy burps. Calder replaced the strap around Ned and helped Hugo to flop over the horse's back, using the tree stump as a stepping block.

From the top of the hill Gwenna saw the boys approaching. Calder didn't need to explain what had happened. When she saw the bedraggled pair and realized that Hugo was in poor shape, she ran on ahead to Hugo's cottage to summon his mother.

Once home, Hugo slid shakily off the horse and his mother brought him inside, stripping off most of his wet clothes onto the flagstone kitchen floor. She slipped a long nightshirt over his head, then pulled off his wet leggings and helped him slide into bed, as Gwenna and Calder ran to the garden and gathered a few sun-warmed stones. Calder placed two at Hugo's feet and Gwenna offered a smaller one for his hands.

"These will warm thee, Hugo," she said softly.

Hugo moaned, clutching the smooth rock to his chest, saying, "Aye, t'is good." His mother brought another woolen blanket to place over him, and he was warm.

"Will he survive?" asked Calder as he and his mother left the cottage.

"Aye, thanks to thee," said Gwenna reassuringly.

"But methinks 'tis me to blame for the accident," confessed Calder with his head bowed low.

"He will be well now, wait and see," said Gwenna in a comforting tone.

Calder returned Ned to Eldred's house as Gwenna walked in the opposite direction towards their own timbered cottage. What had started out as a beautiful day, had somehow gone terribly awry.

On his way home, Calder kicked the dirt at the edge of the lane and saw something black and shiny. He picked up the carbonized rock for good luck and placed it in his leather pouch, running the rest of the way home and whistling for Jack. The kestrel, who had been hovering above the commotion, swooped down to Calder. After returning him to his perch, Calder entered the house to change into his dry bed-shirt for the evening. His wet tunic remained in the moat overnight.

"Did the dog die with him?" was Calder's next inquiry as the family sat around the fireplace. He was talking about his ancestor, Sir John de Thornhill.

"Tis said that the dog pined to death after a week of mourning for his master," explained Gwenna. "When the stone monument was carved, the dog was depicted under his feet like a pillow, which also symbolizes that Sir John was a faithful family man. But now, thou must eat thy supper -- and then to bed."

Calder was ravenous after his long day and his upsetting adventure with Hugo, so he ate heartily, roast pheasant, stuffing, and mashed turnips. After dinner Calder sat at his father's feet by the hearth.

"Think on what thou hast learned today, Calder. Thy mistakes and thy courage are lessons in life," William told him. The fire glowed orange and red. It was the only light in the evening home and they were cozy, warm, and happy as the family settled down for the night.

Calder crawled into bed, closed his eyes, and drifted wearily into a dream. He was worried about Hugo and felt terribly responsible, but he was relieved that his best friend had at least survived the fall and the near drowning.

Now only time would tell.

Iggy Pops and Carbon Rocks

Calder sat bolt upright in the leather chair. Had he slept there all night? Why had his mother not helped him into bed this time? He searched around, but the glove was gone! He looked at the clock and realized that only twenty minutes had passed, yet a whole day in the fifteenth century.

Then Calder remembered and shouted: "Hugo lived! The drowned boy lived!" Jenna ran in to see what the ruckus was about. "Mom, remember the kid who was supposed to have drowned in the moat?" he ranted. "Dave told me about him when we were exploring Thornhill Hall."

"Yes," said Jenna. She remembered the familiar story from when she was growing up in Thornhill. "Anyone who goes down to play at Thornhill Hall hears that story. It keeps kids out of the moat."

"Well, the boy didn't really die. His name was Hugo and he was saved by his good friend Calder, just like me -- and Ned, a horse just like Gallahad."

"Oh, I'm relieved to hear that," she said, semi-sarcastically. "It's worried me ever since I was nine years old."

"No, I'm deadly serious," laughed Calder as he thought about how zany it must sound to others. Try explaining a trip to medieval England when you're still in your pajamas! But had he really been to medieval Thornhill? His question was answered when he stood up to look for the glove and instead, the black rock dropped from a leather pouch on his lap.

"Well, I know for sure that this was not here before," he muttered to himself. "I distinctly remember finding it in the lane on my way home from returning Ned to Eldred. And this is definitely Medieval Calder's leather pouch." Calder took the rock into the living room and showed it to his father.

"Interesting rock Calder. Did you get it in earth science class?"

"No, I found it in medieval -- I mean -- in my bedroom. I think it's coal," replied Calder.

"Let me see," Jenna said, examining the rock. "Yes, it's definitely coal. We used to burn coal in our fireplace when I was growing up in Thornhill. You don't see much of it here in California," she continued. "Did you bring it back from the mining museum?"

Calder shrugged and put the coal in the pocket of his backpack. He planned to share it with Derick and Joe, and maybe even Azule, but right now he was sleepy and needed to snuggle down under his cozy duvet and get some rest.

"G'night, Mom. G'night Dad," he shouted from his room.

"Good night Calder," they called.

At school the first edition of the *Solar Flare* had been a success and people were still requesting copies. Sarah and Jade totaled the proceeds. They had raised $23.75.

"That means some gourmet pizzas and ice-cream sundaes with crimson cherries on top for everyone!" laughed Ellie.

"We may have to raise a little more change to cover that tall order, but we can do it!" added Jade.

Calder's article had been well received and that had made him feel better about being at school. Of course, there were some snide remarks from the people who always gave him a hard time. (Sir Wince-a-lot jokes, etc.) but so what? Calder knew how to ignore them, and the bullies had pretty much left him alone since the last altercation.

At recess Calder pulled out the piece of coal and showed it to Derick, Joe, and Azule, but they weren't as impressed as they had been with the gauntlet.

"What is it?" asked Joe. "How do we know you didn't find it at the beach?"

"Does it look like a beach pebble to you?" snapped Calder, feeling slightly defensive.

"Well no, but it doesn't look too special either," retorted Joe.

"The only thing special about it, is that it somehow came back with me through time, because I distinctly remember kicking it out of the dirt almost five-hundred-fifty years ago. In Thornhill!" Calder insisted. They all laughed, but had to agree that it was pretty mind-boggling, if it were true.

"Perhaps it fell from your nose while you were sleeping in the chair," scoffed Joe.

"Pretty big for a nose booger!" laughed Derick.

Calder slipped it back into his backpack and changed the subject.

"Anyone want a game of wall-ball?"

"I'm up first," Joe volunteered.

Azule walked over to where Ellie was braiding Maddy's long brown hair. "The boys are on a *time warp* adventure," she announced. Ellie made fun by imitating the *Twilight Zone* music, then resumed braiding.

"I want to go with them to medieval England," announced Azule.

"That would be awesome. I could be Juliet," said Maddy. "O, Romeo, Romeo! Wherefore art thou, Romeo?"

"Wasn't that in Italy?" asked Azule.

"It would be cool to dress in those maiden's dresses and wear tall hats with chiffon trailing from the point," continued Maddy, regardless.

"And meet a noble knight on a white stallion," added Ellie.

"I'd shout from the highest tower," continued Azule. "Help save me!" They were instantly saved from their reveries by the end of recess bell.

Several days had gone by since Calder had visited the past and he hadn't had too much time to think about it, but that night he picked up his guitar and began to strum, trying to find the chords from ballads he'd heard in medieval Thornhill:

> Ear-lee one mor-or-ning
> Just as the sun was ri-i-sing,
> I heard a mai-den sing-ing
> In the va-a-lee below.

He'd only had a six-week guitar course with Mr. Mitchell, so he struggled with it, but came fairly close:

"Oh, don't de-cei-eive me,
Oh, ne-ver lea-eave me.
How could you woo-oo a-a poor mai-den so!"

Calder completed it poorly but, "Hey, what the heck," he grumbled as he strummed. "It's a bit too sappy for me anyway, but all the lads sang it in medieval Thornhill." He tried another one that Hugo was singing before they left for Sandal:

Mor-ning hath bro-ken,
Like the first mor-ning.
Black bird hath spo-ken,
Like the first bird.
Praise for the sing-ing,
Praise for the morn-ing.
La..La..La..Laah..La,
La..La..La..Laah.

He couldn't remember some of the lyrics, so he strummed in the blanks and gave up the effort just as his mom came in.

"That sounded pretty good, Calder. I didn't know Mr. Mitchell was teaching you English ballads." She applauded his effort.

Calder put down his guitar and picked up the video controller; compliments made him uncomfortable. He had hoped to be transported back to check on how Hugo was faring, back to the huge open fireplace and the smells of fresh bread. Back where his medieval mother, Gwenna, might be embroidering, and his Father would most certainly be sprawled in his chair in front of the fire with his stocking feet upon a stool, the surface of which might be elaborately embroidered by Gwenna.

"What's missing here, besides the fire hearth?" he asked himself. He looked into the living room at his father. Yes, he too was sprawled on the couch, with his feet up after a tiring day's work, watching the news. Same, yet here everything seemed so disjointed, like looking through the fisheye lens. Everyone was in a separate bubble, doing their own thing. They still communicated through the thin transparent membrane, but then went right back to their separate bubble. Each had a deadline, *Rush, rush, rush*, and *Push, push, push. Do your homework*, and *Get to baseball on time!* -- Leaves no time to stop and smell the bread baking, thought Calder.

However, when the weekend came, Calder decided that he would travel no more. As much as he loved medieval Thornhill, he needed time to ponder and digest all his wanderings to date.

A few weeks rolled by and the lump of coal lay hidden in his backpack. For the time being, he was just too busy to care. Outta sight -- outta mind, he thought dismissively. Yet, occasionally he yearned for the simple country life: kids playing in the fields in the wind and the rain, a cast of hawks flying overhead, and galloping on the back of a real shire horse with only a blanket as a saddle. It all seemed so effortless there. He longed to wear a knight's gleaming armor, and to carry his wooden lance and shield into the jousting arena to face his medieval brother, Sir Jordan de Thornhill.

Here nobody can play during the week because of homework, and when we do play, we tend to sit immobile doing thumb exercises on the video controls, he griped. (More like a parent!) He did enjoy bouncing on the trampoline and riding the go-cart circuit in Adam's back yard, but they hadn't done that for a while. These days, Adam usually hung out with the boys from his own school, while Calder enjoyed surfing or exploring the canyon with Derick and Joe.

He felt around for the chunk of coal, examined it closely, then returned it to the backpack pocket. He would know when the time was right. Bored and frustrated, Calder flopped backwards onto his bed. It was hard being an only child and having to come up with his own entertainment. He pulled a book from the bookshelf and started to read, but he was restless, so he jumped up and put a sprinkle of fish food into the aquarium, then went outside to feed his iguanas.

Clyde was ten years old and was over four feet long from her nose to the tip of her tail. Calder pulled on his gloves and gently lifted her, supporting her around the chest and letting her hind legs straddle his forearm. He set her free in the back yard to cruise around, marveling at how prehistoric she looked, lurching along and climbing rocks. Since Clyde was old, that was as much freedom as she was allowed, for her own safety. Young, agile Rocky, however, had escaped every year in early spring and had lived in the big pepper tree in the backyard until the weather turned cold in November. Calder would then retrieve him to spend the winter in the comfort and warmth of their reptilarium. It was a happy set-up, and since Rocky rarely ventured farther than the tree, Calder now opened the door for him each spring and gave him his freedom. One time, however, he had crossed the street to a neighbor's bush. The neighbor thought her kids were trying to trick her with a rubber lizard -- until he moved, that is! The whole neighborhood heard her scream.

After ten minutes Calder picked Clyde up, returned her to the reptilarium with Rocky, and fed them a handful of fresh dandelion leaves.

"I'll set you free tomorrow Rocky," promised Calder, setting Clyde down on the heated rock inside the cage. "But wait, this is Friday," he thought, securing the door and running back into the house. "Mom, can Derick spend the night?"

"You have baseball *Opening Day* tomorrow morning at eight, but Derick can spend the night if he doesn't mind getting up early," replied Jenna.

"Thanks Mom, we always wake up at 6:30 on weekends," he said enthusiastically. "Could we order a pizza?"

"Yes, that sounds fine," agreed Jenna. Calder called Derick and was pleased to hear that he could come over. His friends always brought their own sleeping bags when they had sleepovers, so Jenna pulled the extra mattress out from under Calder's bed and laid it in the middle of the floor. Derick arrived, followed closely by the pizza man.

Ah, life was good again! Calder had been rescued from the depths of despair! The boys laughed and chatted about the upcoming camp. Now that was something to look forward to -- camping in the mountains with round-the-clock kids. Hopefully, they would be separated from the Cody creeps.

Calder once again examined the piece of black coal. Just to be sure, he checked that it hadn't fallen from his geology project, where twenty samples of different rocks were glued to a chart. Nope, there they were. Twenty samples of sedimentary, igneous, and metamorphic rocks -- all present and correct!

Calder considered telling Derick about his latest adventure, but realized he would probably make fun of it again, so he tossed the coal onto the shelf next to his Norman helmet and flicked on the video game. He knew that when the time was right he would attempt to use the coal to revisit medieval Thornhill.

It might not be tonight, but it would be soon!

OVER EXPOSURE

It was pitch black and there was no air. Calder strained his eyes to see, trying to make sense of where he was, but he could see nothing. It felt like the inside of the *camera-obscura*, but smelled of soot, more like the inside of a chimney. He heard a high-pitched twittering. The finches, he thought, but the pitch was more trill like a canary. Calder's hands and knees ached from the unforgiving ground that he was crawling upon; his body felt cold and thin. For a moment he remembered -- the coal! I should not have used that chunk of coal. If this is Thornhill, it's not the Thornhill I know.

At that moment the twenty-first century dissipated, like steam from a tea kettle, as the fire in his lungs and relentless pain in his body became the norm.

"Get back t' work, lad," shouted a pair of white eyes, which was all that Calder could see of the man up ahead. "Fill yer wagon!" barked the eyes again. As Calder's vision adjusted to the darkness, he could make out more of the figure. There was a dim yellow lantern flickering close by, but the figure was covered from head to toe in black coal dust. Eyes without a face inside a black tunnel.

Calder unloaded his basket into the wagon, dipping his head so that the coal rolled out of the basket on his back. He felt a brief moment of relief as the weight was lifted from his spine.

"Fill yer basket again, Lad!" shouted the dreaded voice, belonging to *the eyes*. Calder coughed and spit black phlegm onto the ground in front of himself. The coal dust was everywhere, thick and suffocating.

Tak -- Tak -- Tak, Calder turned to his right and saw the faint outline of a crouched dark figure against the alcove wall, chipping and chiseling at the coal face.

"Father, is that you? Where are we?" whispered Calder in a raspy voice.

"Down t' pit, Lad," came Will's answer as they both resumed their work. Somehow, the piece of coal from the fifteenth century had made a wrong turn across the ages, transporting Calder to the *NINETEENTH* century; a far bleaker era in Thornhill's long history. Calder picked up the chunks of coal his father was chiseling, raised his bony chest, and hurled the pieces over his shoulder into the basket.

"Be strong, Lad. A few more hours and we'll be done for t' day," whispered his father, trying to encourage Calder to endure. But there was no day for them, this was the nineteenth century in a West Yorkshire mining village. Calder was an eleven-year-old boy, a child worker in the coal mine. He would barely see daylight for a whole week, and these were the new and improved standards of the day! At the beginning of the century whole families had lived out their miserable lives, working below ground. Some of them died like blind moles in their subterranean burrows. Babies were tethered to their mothers so they wouldn't get lost in the tunnels, while the mother did the job that Calder was doing now. Calder didn't really feel the benefit of these *improved* conditions, except for the peace of mind he had, knowing that his own mother, Gerty, could at least enjoy the fresh air and an occasional bright, sunny day.

He thought back to his early childhood, to the breezy days of summer when Mother would hang out her washing on the line in the small yard at the back of the house on Combs Hill. The wind would make the shirts flap around like wild, tethered ghosts, and Calder would run through them laughing gleefully. But Calder no longer had time for such daydreaming and this time the eyes just barked: "Lad, if I have to warn you again!..." But what punishment could he give Calder that was worse than he already had?

Calder resumed his coal collecting faster than before. The weight of his load tugged heavily on his shoulders, until once again it was time to empty the basket. He crawled to the wagon, lowered his head, and thrust his buttocks into the air to force the coal to tumble from the basket, over his bowed head, and into the wagon.

His boss, the owner of the white eyes, fastened the wagon handle to the bridle of a pit pony and led it away again. Originally white, the pony was now blackened by coal dust. Calder straightened himself up after the last chunk fell. There was no relief from his torture, yet he endured.

"What day is it, Father?" he whispered.

"It's only Monday, but just a couple more hours and we can go to t' surface for some o' Mother's tasty beef stew. She'll be waiting for us, then we can rest, Son!"

"Only Monday..." Calder groaned and hung his head. The miners worked from 6:00 a.m. to 6:00 p.m., Monday to Friday. Their salaries were a pittance, barely making enough money for food and boots, but the cottage was owned by the colliery, so the rent was subsidized. They survived, barely.

When six o' clock came around, Calder joined the solemn group of weary boys and men as they squeezed themselves into the lift. It rose slowly and creakily to the surface, their eyes straining to adjust to daylight. At the surface they could relish the last few hours of summer daylight, for what it was worth. In winter they went to work in the freezing dark and came home in the freezing dark, seeing daylight only at weekends.

Calder looked around. There had been a thunderstorm and the ground was soaked. The cobblestones reflected the dark gray sky in their smooth, wet surfaces. Thornhill and the surrounding countryside appeared to be made of pewter. Dreary streets, gloomy skies, melancholy moods. Calder and his father made their way to the top of Combs Hill and entered the back door of their stone, two-storey cottage. The aromatic smell of stew revived their senses as Gerty welcomed them home. There was no such luxury as a bathroom or hot running water, so they washed their hands and faces at the stone sink in the kitchen corner. When they did take a bath, it was in a large zinc tub, brought into the living room and hidden by a screen in front of the fire; the water had to be heated over the coals. Each person would take their turn, while the others busied themselves elsewhere. There wasn't much privacy, but there was respect.

Gerty was always happy to see them. Her day was filled with the monotony of housework and cooking, so she welcomed their quiet evening chats around the oak dining table. Most nights, however, it was all they could do to drag their weary bodies up to bed right after dinner, knowing that they would have to wake up at 5:30 again in order to start another grueling day below ground. This was one such evening, so Gerty cleared the table after their dinner, washed the dishes, packed their lunch boxes, and sat down to knit for a while before going upstairs to bed.

Calder lay on his bed and closed his gritty eyes. This was a miserable existence, especially for an eleven-year-old. He coughed again, his lungs were fiery like a dragon's breath and his ribs ached, but he fell asleep instantly as the candle flame grew dim and eventually extinguished itself.

He woke up early and peered out of his small sash window. This was a dreary summer's day in Thornhill, July 4th 1893! All Calder saw that day was the gray street, the gray sky, and the relentless pouring rain. On the distant horizon, beneath the indigo clouds, shone a slit of pale morning light -- the crack of dawn. He pulled on his work clothes and descended the wooden staircase into the one room below that served as living room, dining room, kitchen, and bathroom. The toilet was outside across the alley. Imagine that on a stormy night!

Mother had prepared ham sandwiches and pickled onions for their lunches. Her freshly-baked apple & blackberry pie had cooled overnight in the pantry. They had been too tired to enjoy it the previous night, so Calder cut two slices, wrapped each slice in wax paper, and placed them in their lunch boxes. He was filling a flask with water from the faucet when his father appeared at the bottom of the stairs. They pulled on their clog boots, donned their wool coats and flat caps, and quietly left the house. Gerty slept on.

Moments later, Will and Calder were descending the mine shaft with their fellow workers, each nodding a silent greeting, or grunting "Ey-up!", then staring at the floor with downcast eyes, as the lift shuddered into the belly of the deep mine.

Calder's day was much like the last, back-breaking and repetitive, emptying basket after basket into the coal wagon. He was looking forward to his lunch when the twittering canary stopped. Calder didn't notice the silence, but he did notice a slight smell of gas. He coughed. Then, there was a huge **BOOM** and a blinding light, too bright for his unadjusted pupils. A green flash followed, then yellow flames were sent scorching and spiraling down the tunnel, turning everything into a blazing inferno.

The roaring flames by-passed their little alcove, but Calder and his father couldn't escape; all the oxygen seemed to be sucked out to feed the fire. The alcove's support beams and the coal above collapsed on top of Calder and Will. They were trapped in a tiny pocket in the seam of coal. Unconscious or dead? There was darkness upon black and it was impossible to tell.

It was the worst disaster in Thornhill's long history. The seventeenth century had seen the fire at Thornhill Hall, where a few of the King's Loyalists had been burned, but this was worse, far worse.

Gerty held her breath in anguish as she met with other

mothers and wives at the face of the colliery that day. They clung to each other as the coal dust had clung to their loved ones' fingernails.

"Unbelievable Tragedy," wrote one reporter. "139 Souls Lost!" wrote another, and over the next few days the headlines read: "Gas to Blame in Pit Explosion", and: "Catastrophic Colliery Disaster at Thornhill".

Had the boss been more attentive, he would have noticed that the canary had stopped singing and was already dead, signaling the presence of poisonous gases. At least they'd have had a few precious moments to get into the lift shaft and rise 425 feet to the safety above ground.

As most of the male population of Thornhill was wiped out in the disaster, help was brought in from the neighboring towns of Dewsbury and Horbury. Once again, men and boys worked tirelessly, side by side, to bring out the victims. It was a morbid sight. Their corpses were laid out on wet, gray cobblestones, covered with gray woolen blankets, and drenched by the relentless rain.

Days passed and still the digging went on. Calder and Will hadn't been found. Gerty was beginning to believe that they never would be, but she never gave up hope. She was desperate to find them alive, because she didn't want to have to look at the agony on their faces, the way the other widows had done with their loved ones.

Would their graves be four-hundred-twenty-five feet below the surface? Was there any chance of survivors?

On July 7th, 1893, the local newspaper reported:
Day Three, "Seven Found Clinging to Life!"

Unholy Hoots

Calder had been feverish for three days. Jenna took his temperature: 103.4 degrees Fahrenheit. It was high! She wet a wash cloth with cold water, wrung it out, and placed it on Calder's forehead, then offered him a sip of water through a bendy straw.

"Try to take a tiny sip every few minutes," she whispered. Calder opened his eyes and cooperated.

"Ah, I needed that," he mumbled. "The fire was so hot, so-o-o hot..." he trailed off weakly. His cheeks were crimson and his hair was tousled around his face.

"You have a fever, Calder," said Jenna, feeling quite concerned. He had been this way before. Usually, by the third day the fever would break, and then a runny nose or a cough would take over from the fever.

Jenna was a naturalist; she believed that the body needed to overheat in order to kill the virus, so she preferred to avoid fever reducers, except if his temperature rose above 103.5 degrees. She also held on to the old saying: *starve a fever, feed a cold,* so she offered only clear drinks during the fever stage. The cool compress seemed to be working, and the next time Jenna looked into Calder's bedroom he was sleeping soundly and his cheeks weren't quite so crimson anymore.

By afternoon Calder announced, "I feel much better now, but I have a scratchy throat and a runny nose." Jenna was relieved; it seemed to be a cold virus after all and now he was over the high fever.

Calder sat up in bed, his pillow damp from sweat and from the wet compress. He remembered his dream, or had it been real? He searched for the piece of coal, but it was gone. He shuddered as a chill ran up his spine.

"I should never have gone back!" he gasped. "I will never, ever, try that again!" His coal mining disaster had shaken him to his core and he was so glad to be back home in his own California bed. "I'm hungry, Mom!" he bellowed hoarsely, then coughed.

Almost over the worst, thought Jenna. She re-checked his temperature, 100.2 degrees F. "You'll be able to have some toast soon," she said, "but for now, have another sip of water, Love."

Calder had been absent for several days, but he was now feeling well enough to return to school. Talk at school was focused on sixth-grade camp. Every year busloads of sixth-graders headed up into the mountains for a week of fun. This year it had almost been cancelled, due to the fact that in the previous autumn Southern California had practically burned to a cinder. The campsite had not been spared; everything there had burned. The camp cabins had since been rebuilt along with new picnic tables and a new mess hall. Camp would prevail! Wild fires usually occurred in October after the long, hot summers when the grasses and trees were really dry, but now it was spring and the chances of fire were pretty low.

The sixth grade kids were excited. Calder had never spent a whole week away from home, but he figured it would be no different than spending time in another era. If he could handle that, he could handle anything. He decided to pick out his own clothes for camp. Jenna had written a *suggestions list* and he also conferred with Derick and Joe, who agreed that being comfortable and warm were top priority.

They were allowed two bags: One full of clothes and the other containing a pillow, a sleeping bag, and a towel. Calder consulted his mom's list, but it was way too long. He packed just half of Jenna's suggestions along with a tiny sketchbook and pencils. Last but not least, he stuffed the soft leather pouch into the side pocket of the bag. Just for luck, and to remind him: I am a *Knight-in-Training* -- and I will survive!!

Calder thought of Hugo and hoped that he'd survived the near drowning incident. Knowing there were no antibiotics in the fifteenth century, he hoped he hadn't developed a lung infection from the moat water. His chances seem pretty good. They have excellent natural cures there, he reassured himself, remembering Dave with the stinging nettle cure.

He thought about the other Calder and his father trapped underground in the nineteenth century and hoped they had been among the survivors. What a terrible life and a tragic accident, he sighed as he wondered: Could there be a boy just like me in every era?

The clock on Calder's bedroom wall ticked loudly, he was having trouble falling asleep. He put the thoughts of the colliery disaster out of his mind; it was too painful a memory. He turned his thoughts instead to sixth-grade camp. He was excited, yet apprehensive. He hoped he would be grouped with Derick and Joe, because although the situation had improved slightly at school, he was still an *outsider* with a lot of the other kids. At ten o' clock, Calder's mind was still full of turmoil. He switched on his I-pod and listened to his favorite band, TYR, a Faroese folk/metal band. Very Viking, very cool! His mind became calmer as his thoughts began to drift once again to the old country.

He wondered if he would ever be able to go back there, to the right place and the right era. His confidence had been shaken by the last trip, but now he realized that he had made a grave mistake in using the piece of coal. Although he'd found the coal in fifteenth century Thornhill, he had somehow been transported to the coal mine of nineteenth century Thornhill, the right place, but definitely the wrong time. When he had used the Norman helmet, he'd been transported neither to present day Whitby, nor to the Norman era. That time, he'd been successful in arriving in the medieval era, but strangely enough, in the town where he'd purchased the helmet. Hmmmm! Calder realized that there were no guarantees with this time-travel business. All he knew was, if there was a next time, he must stay on course by holding or wearing something that was truly indigenous to fifteenth century Thornhill. With this thought, Calder eased into a pleasant slumber and slept undisturbed until the morning light spread in diagonal stripes through his blinds and onto his blue duvet.

The school buses formed a yellow train beside the red curb, in front of the entrance to the school. The loud chatter escalated as more and more sixth-graders arrived at their designated departure zones. Several parents and teachers milled amongst the crowd. Some of the first-timers had anxious looks on their faces, but most of the children were quite excited. The adventure was about to begin. Maddy, Ellie, and Azule had already found each other when Sarah and Jade arrived.

Sarah's dark brown eyes flashed around the crowd and connected with one friend after another; she was bubbling over with excitement. Even Azule's relative calmness was sporadically broken by an excited wave, a smile, and a flash of her brilliant blue eyes. If Calder was excited, it didn't show.

Calder, Derick, and Joe were the first to climb onto the bus; they made a bee-line for the back seat. On the way down the aisle, Calder stopped to open a window.

"Fresh air -- we need fresh air," he announced in a panicky, claustrophobic manner. Small closed spaces now reminded him of his painful memories in the coal mine disaster. The bus filled quickly. Two teachers were assigned to each bus; they'd be spending the week at camp with the kids.

"Find your places," said Mr. Mitchell as he alighted the first bus. Azule, Ellie, and Maddy were also assigned to the same bus as the boys and found their seats about midway down, while Sarah and Jade joined their group on the second bus.

Cody Kenyon headed towards the back seat and

glared at Calder, Joe, and Derick. Calder was expecting another confrontation, but they just sat tight and Cody said nothing. His power over Calder seemed to have been diffused recently. In fact, Mr. Mitchell recognized the potential situation and sent Cody and his cohorts onto the other bus, and apart from a couple of snarls here and there, Cody Kenyon barely bothered Calder again.

As the buses pulled away from the curb, Calder looked out of the back window and waved to his mom. By writing with an imaginary pen on her open left hand, she motioned for him to write. Calder nodded in agreement as the bus pulled out of the driveway and headed down the street, but of course, he'd forget to write.

The bus made its way through the affluent town of Rancho Santa Fe, passing orange groves, hibiscus hedges, white ranch-style fences, horse paddocks, and grand elaborate driveway entrances with sweeping palms and eucalyptus trees. They drove on, past the depleted reservoir, where you could see the old waterline high above the lake. To Calder this journey was a familiar one; his grandparents owned a cabin in the mountains. When the fires had burned, the old gold-mining town of Julian had barely been spared; the fires burned on three sides of the quaint little town. Calder's grandparents hadn't known until weeks later whether or not their summer cabin had survived. Many people had lost their homes and all of their possessions, their horses and other pets; in fact, everything! His grandparents never complained, especially as there were others less fortunate than themselves. After the disaster, they were happy to find that their cabin had been spared, but the fire had come within half a mile of it.

On past the Wild Animal Park, the scenery was changing and becoming more rural, vineyards spread out on either side of the road. Calder pointed to an ostrich farm on the right and everybody became excited. It was a humorous sight, those huge birds with their little heads and big eyes, long necks, fluffy black bodies, and humongous dinosaur legs, all running around in a farmer's field.

"It's Dexter's sister, Dee-Dee, wearing a tutu!" Calder exclaimed. Joe and Derick laughed at the cartoon connection.

The bus continued up the mountainous pass, through high plains and the quaint western-style towns of Ramona and Santa Ysabel. They saw areas where fire-charred trees looked like gnarled, black bony hands reaching out from the desolate, gray earth. Little green spears of grass were beginning to sprout from the charred earth, making the apocalyptic scene look a little more hopeful.

Eventually, the buses arrived at their destination. The students poured out and were divided into packs, such as: Coyote, Red Fox, Mountain Lion, and -- "Grape!" volunteered Calder, showing his blissfully ridiculous sense of humor.

The cabins were divided up into four rooms with a hallway running down the middle. Calder, Joe, Derick, Steve, and several other boys were assigned to Red Fox den. Calder took his first look inside. A row of bunks aligned each side of the room and two facing him at the bottom of the room.

"Let's grab the far end bunks," suggested Joe, peering over Calder's shoulder. All were in favor, so they ran and threw themselves on their beds. Joe and Calder were the first to grab the top bunks, and Steve and Derick slid underneath to the bottom bunks. Calder tested his bed for bounce-ability, but it scored pretty low.

Calder was relieved to see that the Cody creeps were assigned to Coyote den. He wasn't afraid of them, he just didn't need the constant annoyance. Who would? He unrolled his sleeping bag, fluffed up his pillow, threw the rest of his tackle into one of the boxes at the end of the bed, and flopped back onto his pillow, ready to enjoy his upcoming adventure.

Several minutes later, the *clang -- clang -- clang* of the lunch bell sounded. There was a flutter of excitement as the eager students gathered around the picnic tables, anticipating food. However, the first items on the agenda were *Camp Rules* and *Regulations*. They had already signed an agreement before their arrival, so they knew what was expected and what was not allowed.

"Pretty much the same as school rules and common sense," commented Jade.

Azule and Ellie were assigned to their den, and Sarah, Maddy, and Jade were together across the hall. Maddy sighed when she split up from Azule and Ellie, but she knew that she was in for some fun with Sarah. The girls' cabins were on the opposite side of the camp from the boys, so there were a lot less distractions and interactions between the groups. However, they did have co-ed eating areas and some co-ed activities, like hikes, archery, bird-watching trips, and sitting around the campfire at night.

By the second day everything at camp was running smoothly. When the bell rang, every person came running to the tables. Because they were exercising so much, they were always famished. Each day took them on an eight-mile hike through the mountain trails and alongside craggy waterfalls, learning all they could about the local flora and fauna.

Calder would quickly pull out his art book and pencil and make a sketch of any new birds, taking note of its plumage, shape, and size. If he heard its call, he would note that too. "Today," he wrote, "a squawking, walnut-cracking band of crested Blue Jays plundered the camp."

Mealtime was the time they could catch their breath and confer with friends, swapping stories of adventure from their morning hike. One group had seen a rattlesnake near a rocky outcrop, but the vigilant counselor was always ahead of the group looking for such dangers, and the students knew not to veer off the open footpath. He told them to stand very still while the rattler slithered away. Then they had been able to pass by carefully and safely.

The best time was evening when they could finally relax, shower, eat, and then gather around the campfire in their cozy sweats, roasting marshmallows, as they took turns telling scary stories and listening to the "whoooo-whooo" of an invisible, ghostly owl. The amber flickering flames cast eerie shadows all about them, making their faces look like spooky Halloween masks. Friends huddled together on the edges of their seats, their eyes wide, anticipating the surprises, shudders, and chills that they hoped would befall them.

Calder took a deep breath, ready to tell his friends about the colliery disaster, but then refrained in case it spoiled their enthusiasm for his tales of medieval England.

He was also reluctant to go through the profound experience again, so he turned his attention to Thornhill

Hall and its deep encircling moat, entwined with ancient history. He threw in an element of woeful, wandering spirits and a mischievous rapscallion poltergeist, just for good measure, while the group of listeners became enthralled:

"It was a dark and stormy night. The deep indigo moat surrounding the manor had lain undisturbed for many centuries..."

Pepperoni Pizza and Dragon Wings

Calder planned a pizza party with an evening of video games. His original plan was to invite Joe, Derick, Steve, Ellie, Maddy, and Azule, but as the time approached he realized that he must invite only those friends who corresponded with their medieval counterparts. So, Joe, Derick, and Azule were invited. Calder had regained his confidence and was preparing to show his friends how their own counterparts lived in medieval England.

"Be prepared for a mind-boggling adventure!" he warned them. They only half believed him, but the stories he had told at camp were out of this world, or more to the point, out of this millennium!

Jenna ordered the largest possible New York-style pizza. When it arrived, it practically took up the whole circular table in the dining room. Calder wanted to eat first, just in case they *warped* during their video game. He didn't want them to be hungry arriving in medieval Thornhill.

After eating pizza and Caesar salads, Jenna served them cookie-dough ice-cream, which definitely threw them all into a sugar spin.

The four played outside in the backyard until the evening mosquitoes threatened to bite, then they hurried to Calder's room to play the one game that Calder believed would transport them all to fifteenth century Thornhill: *ZARKAN!*

The game starts with *Bezok*, a young medieval knight-in-training, plodding through an ancient village, brandishing what appears to be a wooden sword. He wears a green tunic similar to medieval Calder's, and he finds his way to the edge of a dense forest, where foxes and badgers are running wild. His goal is to advance through many tricky obstacles on different levels, in order to find the castle, free the damsel in distress, and become a gallant knight.

Calder had thought in advance about which amulet to use in order to return to Thornhill. Should he use the fragment of chimney stone that his mom had brought back from their first visit to Thornhill Hall when Calder was just two? No! That wouldn't work. He wanted no mistakes! The last place he wanted to end up was Thornhill Hall on the night of the fiery battle. The only object he owned, that had traveled with him from medieval Thornhill, was the leather pouch into which he had slipped the chunk of coal. The pouch that belonged to medieval Calder. That was it! Nothing else would do, but minus the piece of coal, of course!

Calder also realized that in order to take his friends along, they all had to be connected by the video game. He had the *Zarkan* game in two different formats. The screen-based game was for a solo player, but the portable version could be played by up to four people, as long as they connected their systems by cable links. Calder explained his plans to the group, who were now sitting in a tight circle on the spare mattress in the middle of his bedroom floor. He loosened the pouch strings, frantically clearing it of any particles of coal dust, and laid the circular piece of leather in their midst.

"Do you think we should be touching the pouch?" asked Azule, concerned that someone might get left behind.

"I'm a proficient time traveler now. Just stay focused and we'll be okay," commanded Calder, concentrating on the task ahead.

"We could place the tip of our toes on it," murmured Derick nervously, but that seemed a little awkward.

"No need," said Calder confidently. "The amulet is at our center and we're interlinked by the cables. We'll be fine!" Calder cast a hopeful glance around the anxious group as they each held their game systems tightly in their hands. "Here goes," he whispered, while controlling Bezok, the tiny medieval figure, through the villages and forests of the first level. He felt sure the plan would work, but at what point in the game nobody knew.

As he slipped into the dense forest, Bezok encountered the first sly fox. Pretty soon a den of snarling foxes had him surrounded. Calder thought quickly, spun Bezok in a circle with his outstretched sword, and sliced the bloody snouts off each and every one of them. Zzlinng! After several such encounters, Bezok advanced through the forest towards the lake.

"Are we all still here?" panicked Derick after a few minutes.

"Don't have any doubt in your mind!" exclaimed Azule,

trying to keep her focus on the game. "Think positive and just concentrate!"

Bezok battled the giant green pike in the lake. Casting his line like an expert fisherman, he hooked *Walter* firmly by the fish lip and flipped the monstrous aquatic beast onto the grassy bank, thrashing and gulping at the open air. Extricating his boots from the muddy water's edge, Bezok then took a moment to fashion the pike's scaly skin into a shield, before advancing to the new forest on the far side of the lake, in search of the dragon's lair.

A few more minutes went by -- a mutual glance -- still nothing had happened to the group of wannabe time-adventurers. After approximately thirteen minutes of Bezok's meanderings, they had resigned themselves to the fact that they were probably going nowhere, so they became more relaxed and more focused on the game, rather than on their own travel quest. At this precise moment, all four minds were completely engrossed in the game and a split second later they were there, inside the graphics, inside the forest, feeling the trees all around them, inhaling the smell of green moss and fresh dew that hung in the dampness of the cool morning air.

Again their eyes locked and together they let out a surprised gasp. They were there, in Thornhill, standing at the edge of the moat -- and with a bit of luck, they had arrived in the fifteenth century! Calder grasped Joe's arm and led him to the edge of the moat; Azule and Derick followed closely behind them.

"Watch thy step," Thomas cautioned Abigail, who now had no recollection of Derick or Azule. They had all left the twenty-first century behind.

Dawn was breaking through the darkness of the trees. There was no sun, just a dimly lit, misty fog that hung over the swampy moat. Two marble griffins stood at the top of the steps. Gog and Magog, the mythical eagle-headed lions, were crouching upon their pedestals, ready to pounce on any threat.

Hugo broke the silence, "Dost thou remember when I almost drowned in yonder moat? I know not if I properly thanked thee for saving my life."

"Twas I who was at fault for riding so recklessly around the moat, Hugo. Methinks, I should have acted more responsibly," replied Calder. "But 'tis thanks enough that thou art still standing here beside us now," he continued with great relief. "I would not have forgiven myself, had it turned out differently."

Abigail crouched in the mist at the water's edge, her fingers skimming the carpet of lime green duckweed. The tiny plants separated momentarily, revealing the pitch-black water beneath. A shudder ran up her spine; it was eerie! Instinctively, Abigail retreated, allowing the floating carpet of *Lemna minor* to magically repair itself.

"Methinks, I would neither want to breathe nor swallow this mire," she gasped, thinking of Hugo's traumatic experience.

"Aye," agreed Hugo. "Into the bog of eternal stench..." Abigail had recited a few lines of her new poem to them a week earlier. She was impressed that Hugo had remembered the first line.

"Into the bog of eternal stench, rode a wench on a horse-like bench," she chuckled as she added the next line. At last, the somber atmosphere was broken. Abigail fancied herself a philosopher as well as a poet, but she left

the rhyme unfinished as they looked towards the east.

Daylight was now fully surrounding the four young figures. The fog lifted, leaving a thin ghostly mist above the moat, like Avalon at the dawn of time. The manor house was clearly visible now with its gothic stone windows, heavily studded oak door, and impressive broad chimney. Magpies and ravens nested in the surrounding trees and broke the morning stillness with a *Caw -- Caw -- Caw.*

At that point, the farm to the east of the manor came to life too. There were sounds of wooden pails being placed onto the stone workbench, a rooster crowed, and the farmer could be heard harnessing his cart horse to the heavy, V-shaped plough. This wooden tool would be dragged by the horse and steered by the farmer as it gouged a furrow into the soil. The seeds would then be scattered into the furrows by hand. Massive hooves plodded the black, wet soil as Abigail, Calder, Hugo, and Thomas raced to the wall and peered over.

"Heigh-ho, can we work for thee today, Farmer Ibbotson?" they pleaded.

"Aye, there be plenty o' work to do, climb over," answered the white haired, well-weathered farmer. He was always glad of help, since the land now belonged to him and the profits were his to reap. In the old days of the feudal system, farmers worked the land, but all the profits would have gone to the Lord of the manor.

Farmer Ibbotson motioned Abigail and Thomas to go help Dame Ibbotson with her daily chores of feeding hens, collecting eggs, milking cows, and chopping wood. He took the other two boys to where the horse was standing. The horse seemed older and a little slower than Eldred's horse, and this one was chestnut brown. His name? Bob.

Farmer Ibbotson laced his fingers to create a hand stirrup. Hugo placed his left foot in it and Mr. Ibbotson heaved him onto the horse; he did the same for Calder. This time Hugo was in charge of the horse and Calder held onto Hugo's leather belt.

"Ride thee in a straight line all the way down yonder field, then back again to make another long furrow," the farmer directed. He slapped the horse's flank and shouted, "Gidd y'up!" Hugo held the reins tightly and Mr. Ibbotson followed, guiding the "V" of the plough through the earth. It was always exciting to be working, thought Calder. This was the next best thing to being a knight. In the autumn, the boys would help pick potatoes growing in this same field and would be paid a farthing for every five sacks that they filled.

After the field was plowed, they found that today's pay was awaiting them. With Dame Ibbotson's help, Abigail had cooked a hearty breakfast of fried eggs, black-pudding sausage, and mushrooms, served with a hunk of freshly baked bread. They ate well, then Dame Ibbotson sent them home with a fragile package of eggs and mushrooms, tied up in a muslin cloth.

When they reached the top of the hill where Calder's house stood, the four friends separated, each with their little parcels to give to their mothers.

"Let us meet at Kirkfield in one hour," shouted Thomas as they went their separate ways.

"Aye, anon!" they all agreed.

As he entered the cottage, Calder found his mother sewing a new tunic for him. He had grown three inches taller that year. Calder recognized the fabric and the color. It was the finely-woven, Lincoln green wool that

Uncle Eldred had promised him.

"It doth look very fine, Mother!" he said, placing the eggs gently into an earthenware bowl on the table.

Gwenna stood up and draped the tunic in front of him to measure for length. "How handsome thou art, Calder," she remarked proudly.

"Aye, 'tis a fine tunic, alright," replied Calder, deflecting the compliment. He opened the curtain to his bed and flopped onto his mattress. As he rested, his thoughts pondered the future, but not the twenty-first century *space age, digital* world of Millennium Calder. Such a future would have been inconceivable to Medieval Calder. In his world, there weren't even any other modes of transport, except to go by foot, horse, cart, or boat. In his world, the only light in the house was candlelight, fire in the fireplace, or daylight. There certainly were no such things as jets or space shuttles. No skateboards, video games, plasma TV's, DVDs, I-pods, or PC's, and the only type of electricity was that which occurred naturally, static or lightning.

No, the future that Calder was pondering, was his dream of becoming a knight like Sir Jordan and Sir John de Thornhill. Calder vowed to practice his swordsmanship as soon as he'd asked Mr. Bradford about forging him a metal sword to replace his childish wooden one. Calder, Hugo, and Thomas had planned to build a jousting arena in Kirkfield, where they could practice their horsemanship.

Calder ran through the drill in his mind, remembering the lesson he'd had with Sir Jordan. He pictured himself upon the back of a chestnut mare with a long flowing tail and mane. He checked his feet in the stirrups and sat tall. In place of his soft leather boots, he imagined the articulated scales of armor and felt the weight of the helmet upon his head. As he adjusted his imaginary shield, he drifted into a dream:

Calder roamed the meadows and heavily forested slopes looking for a castle to defend. Trotting through golden wheat fields and past craggy waterfalls, he eventually discovered a place to rest, next to an ancient wooden footbridge. His horse was also glad of the rest, for they had ventured far and wide, and had traveled for more than a day in his dream time.

The young knight took off his helmet and placed it on the rocky outcrop, where his horse was happily chomping grass. He leaned his shield against the rock formation and knelt down, cupping his hands to drink from the clear, frigid stream. As Calder knelt, the heavy armor disappeared as if by magic and he felt comfortable in his new Lincoln green tunic. He pulled his long velvet cape around his shoulders and looked across the small, wooden bridge to where a castle gleamed in the mid-day sun. Several pointed flags were batting in the breeze and seemed to beckon him, come hither. Calder scanned the narrow windows of the towers and turrets in search of a damsel in distress, but was relieved to find that there was none.

Tseeeeeeah -- Tseeeeeeeah, the piercing shriek of a falcon called from above. Calder's eyelids twitched furiously as he scanned the cerulean sky in his dream. His eyes settled upon a tiny black speck high above the meadow, he whistled his high-pitched call and the speck grew larger, until he could make out the mottled underbelly of his own kestrel, Jack. Calder stretched out his arm and adjusted his hand, which was now magically sporting a leather gauntlet.

With Jack landing expertly on the outstretched glove, Calder wove the jesses firmly between his fingers. Then with his left hand, he deftly slipped the leather hood over the kestrel's eyes and secured it gently onto his head, keeping the bird calm and under control. Calder's voice was soft; he told Jack how pleased he was to see him. He told him to be prepared to serve as his master's eyes. Sir Calder would need the kestrel to scour the land for him in search of great adventure.

At that moment Calder heard a voice. "Heigh-ho, art thou laiking, Calder?" It was Hugo. Calder had overslept and had forgotten that they'd all planned to meet in Kirkfield.

"Aye, anon," replied Calder groggily. "Alas, I must have drifted into a faraway dream," he explained apologetically.

Abigail had accompanied Hugo and Thomas; she was admiring the new green tunic as she chatted to her Aunt Gwenna.

"Mother is making for me a gown of indigo velvet with pointed sleeves at the wrists," she announced proudly. "Methinks, I might like to wear it for the May Day festival."

"Ah, that will look elegant with thy beautiful blue eyes, Abigail," said Gwenna. "And how thou hast grown! Just a few more years and thou wilt be fully grown." Abigail smiled proudly and checked herself coquettishly in the mirror. She already felt like a young woman when she was with her aunt, but for now she still had more playing to do. She skipped joyfully over to where the boys were standing.

"Race thee to Kirkfield," coaxed Abigail, but Calder said he was still quite drowsy and preferred to amble along.

"My body doth seem to be still in dreamland," he said groggily.

Abigail had brought her poem written on parchment to show her aunt, but had completely forgotten about it. It was tied around her wrist with a fine, burgundy ribbon. The young maiden was happy to walk demurely along, checking her posture and smiling gracefully at passers-by. It wasn't until they entered Kirkfield from the churchyard that she dropped the pseudo-sophistication and broke into a run.

"Be there any knight brave enough to defend their Queen and country?" rallied Abigail fervently.

"We shall defend thee!" shouted Thomas and Hugo enthusiastically.

"Aye, as will I!" yelled Calder. Now fully awake, he vaulted with ease onto the wall in front of Abigail. "The dragon hath yet to be slain," Calder declared valiantly. "Show us the location of yonder lair."

Their favorite tales were those of *Saint George and the Dragon, King Arthur and the Knights of the Round Table,* and *Guinevere, daughter of King Loedigrance of Camelot*. On this occasion, Hugo immersed himself in the role of Gallahad, and Calder was the kind, yet brave Lancelot.

Thomas joined Calder on the stone wall. "I be Sir Bedevere thy Grace, and I shall defend thee from ye fiery dragon." They were all eager to impress their Guinevere. And last but by no means least, the gigantic haystack took on the unfortunate role of the fearsome, fiery dragon.

The dragon's huge size and great power almost eclipsed the pale blot of an English sun as the knights stared into its gaping, scarlet throat at the blazing inferno inside. The dragon's massive spiked tail, scaly serpentine back, and hideous cruel claws almost overwhelmed the three young knights. A pair of demonic, lurid eyes glared down at them furiously for having been so rudely awakened, yet they fought on bravely.

Suddenly, the fearsome, trembling beast raised its gargantuan head, opened its gaping jaws, and emitted a fiery, rumbling, foul blast of halitosis-ridden breath. Lancelot and Gallahad tumbled madly backwards onto the ground. The imaginary beast reared up a second time, this time bellowing, screaming, and smothering them with a suffocating black smoke, but the brave young knights refused to surrender. Springing back into action, the trio lurched furiously forward, brandishing their weapons and charging like a band of berserk barbarians towards the beast. Having synchronized their next attack, the young knights struck the cruel dragon in the soft area of the neck, right below the jaw. Its wings quivered madly, its eyes bulged bulbously, and finally, with an earth-shattering crash, the once ferocious dragon succumbed and folded at their feet.

By the end of the afternoon, many a golden serpentine scale had been struck violently from the dragon's flesh and lay scattered in clumps all around its limp and lifeless body -- the haystack demolished! Abigail gazed in amazement at the slain dragon, while applauding and congratulating her knights for their true bravery.

"My champions, my heroes!" she called dramatically, holding her poem as if it were a proclamation. Thomas sounded the trumpet of victory: Ter -- Ter -- Er! After which, the three knights collapsed simultaneously and lay laughing on the ground. Hugo decided to go a step further by faking a dramatic death. Thrusting the sword into his side, he buckled over into a near somersault. Then Calder, lying at right angles to him, and not wanting to be outdone by his friend's dramatic exit, stabbed himself through the heart and twisted the sword violently, as he lay thrashing and twitching on the ground for several Shakespearean moments.

"Not such a befitting end for my gallant, brave knights!" proclaimed Abigail, with both hands on her hips, and an air of disappointment. But then, overtaken by her great loss, she feigned a very dramatic, yet graceful faint and slid like a wilting flower from the wall to the ground, about three feet away from the pile of knights.

A moment later, Azule sat up grinning and looked over at the pile of boys. Joe, Derick, and Calder were laughing hysterically on the mattress in Calder's room -- in the TWENTY-FIRST century! The *Zarkan* game had been defeated, the damsels saved, and the consoles and cables lay intertwined on the mattress between the boys. But they all knew there was more to it than that.

Azule exploded with uncharacteristic ebullience. "I saw medieval England," she fizzed. "We were all there -- together -- in Kirkfield!"

"What the heck are you talking about?" gasped Calder. For a split second, Azule feared that she'd been the only one to experience it. Her eyes grew wild with shock. Then Calder added, "Trick! Yes! We were there! We were, without a doubt, in medieval England, Azule!"

The boys sat up and grinned at each other. After his last disaster, Calder was clearly relieved not to have lost a friend on the journey, but he wanted to check that they had all experienced the same adventure.

"What was my mother's name in medieval Thornhill?"
"Aunt Gwenna," replied Azule.

"What did you see at the moat?" Calder inquired further. They all described the scene perfectly.

"What chores did you do, and what was the farmer's name?" They all knew immediately what Calder was talking about and described the chores that each had done for the farmer and Dame Ibbotson.

"ABSO-bloomin'-LUTELY we did it!" cried Calder. The leather pouch was still on the mattress beneath their feet. Calder heaved a heavy sigh and blew the air slowly out from between his pursed lips. It was PHEN-OM-ENAL! The four were now linked with each other in a way that they had never imagined before; they were connected by history.

Azule was sitting in the black leather swivel chair. As she stood up, a small, rolled piece of parchment tied with a burgundy ribbon, fell to her feet. She picked it up and began to read. Although she wasn't sure she fully understood it, she was elated.

"It's Abigail's poem!" she announced with an air of disbelief. "May I publish it in the next issue of the Solar Flare?" she pleaded.

Calder looked at her seriously and replied, "Azule, it's yours. Yours and Abigail's. You are one and the same!" A synchronized shudder ran up each and everyone's spine. "What's yours is hers and vice versa. *Grasp both ends and hold on tight*..." he quoted from the penultimate line of her poem.

Azule smiled and looked down at the parchment in her hands. "Look who's the philosopher, now!" she laughed. "But then, how could this possibly be?" she muttered as she remembered writing the lines nearly five and a half centuries ago.

It was a wonderful catalyst between the pre-teens. What knowledge they had learned through the past! They would spend weeks proposing different theories for what had happened. All were interesting, but none was definite. They vowed to keep their adventure a secret, because they doubted anyone would believe their magnificent tale, and they now understood what Calder had been up against earlier.

At school, their studies seemed more interesting, especially social studies. They had personally experienced history first-hand -- another time, another place, another self!
They all scored well in their final grades, but best of all, they each now had three exceptional friends.

DOUBLE BUBBLE SCOOPS

Sixth grade was fast approaching its end. The next *Solar Flare* was being released to coincide with the annual *May Social*, which was a great success every year. After that, all the students had to look forward to was their graduation day, then the long-awaited summer leading up to the great unknown -- junior high.

Most families participated in the May Social, donating their time or items for the silent auction or the book sale. Alternatively, they might bake a cake for the cake walk. It was organized with the intention of raising funds to update computers, or to buy equipment for the new science and art labs. In addition, it was the most fun day of the whole school year.

Calder woke up early, ready for a fun-filled day. Jenna had already loaded the car with the painted *wave* backdrop and was struggling to fit the surfboard into the trunk. She had scoured the thrift shops in search of a recyclable surfboard and had been successful in finding one with a chunk missing out of the rear end, even the fin was gone. No good for surfing, but it made a perfect photo prop. Calder's dad had secured it with heavy bolts to a wooden base. The nose of the board was protruding out of the trunk, so Calder taped a red rag to the tip, then they were ready to go.

Other set-up volunteers were arriving as Jenna's car pulled up at the curb. Calder knew where to find a ladder; he had done this job six years in a row. They had two hours before the ten o' clock deadline to create all kinds of stages, stalls, auctions, and fun activities. Janitors and parents synchronized their plans over walkie-talkies and cell phones. Coffee and fresh pastries were served, and by ten it was as though this cool school faire had always existed, just like the market cross at Thornhill.

Jenna climbed the ladder to secure her backdrop to the top of the wall, Calder positioned the surf board at an angle in front of the wave, then Jenna draped the aqua-colored fabric under the nose of the board and down onto the ground all around it, to hide the cement and to emulate the surf.

"How about a test shot?" requested Jenna, switching on the digital camera. Calder took off his shoes and shirt, so the photo would look more authentic, then he hopped onto the board and struck a surfer pose. Jenna zoomed in to crop out the surrounding wall, focused on Calder, then took the shot.

"One more," she said, as Calder precariously *hung-ten* off the nose of the board, which started to tip forward. He hopped back to the center of the board for balance, and Jenna decided to place another heavy cinder block on the back end of the base, carefully hiding it under the fabric. Calder tried the pose again and this time it worked. He positioned his toes over the nose of the board and arched his back, *hanging-ten* just as Joe had done in the class.

"Okay, thanks Calder. Super shot," declared Jenna, checking the image. Calder and the board appeared to pop right out of the tubular wave.

Joe's mom was working in the multi-media room. She was downloading and printing the images from the computer. Azule had volunteered to help on the first shift. Her job was to insert the printed photos into card frames and present them to the customers. It felt a bit like being back in the photography class.

Calder had money in his pocket and he was ready to rock n' roll. His first destination was the ticket booth, followed by the *Dunk Tank*. Students lined up for the opportunity to dunk Ms. Dawson, the school Principal, into the tank of cold water. Calder looked her right in the eyes and smiled mischievously. He took aim at the circular release-lever and pitched the ball as he would in his baseball game. *Ker-splash!* The planks opened downward and gravity did the rest. Ms. Dawson was in the tank, soaked! All the kids cheered as she bobbed to the surface in her black wetsuit.

"What a good sport!" thought Jenna as the Principal pushed the planks back into a horizontal position, pulled herself back up onto them, and prepared herself for the next plunge.

"Better than the turnip shy at Thornhill!" exclaimed Calder, heading for higher ground.

When all their volunteer work was done, the four accomplished *Time-Surfers* gravitated towards each other. Azule found Derick first as she was leaving the used book stall.

"I bought a great book," she announced. "Now let's see if we can find Calder and Joe." The sun was scorching down on the red-shouldered population; by mid-afternoon several necks were glowing a deep shade of crimson. Calder was sitting high on the cement steps overlooking the May Day crowd when Azule caught sight of him.

"Calder, we've been looking all over for you. What are you doing up here?" she asked.

"I was observing time -- and trying to figure out how we crossed over into medieval Thornhill," answered Calder pensively.

"Well, I found a book on medieval castles and Sandal is in it. Look!" Azule said, thrusting the book into Calder's hands. She plunked herself down beside him, and they started flicking through the pages until they found the photograph of a section of ruined castle, a mound, and half a round tower.

"Not much left of it, is there?" sighed Calder. "Sir Jordan would most definitely be disappointed to see that time had reduced it to this pile of rubble."

Derick found Joe and they arrived together at the top of the steps.

"What do you think of time?" Calder asked as they sat down alongside Azule.

"It's about two o' clock," answered Joe.

"No, I mean space/time continuum, etc.," Calder clarified.

"All I know is that it speeds up when I'm having fun and slows to a crawl when I'm waiting for school to end!" offered Derick.

"So true!" agreed Joe. "What's the latest theory, Calder?"

Calder proposed that time could have many forms. "You know how light has a duality of particles and waves, right?" he began. "And how it can bend or split as it passes through a prism?"

"Yeah, like that cool prism in the photography class," declared Joe.

"The wind can be a gentle breeze, a howling gale, or a ferocious hurricane, too..." added Azule poetically.

"But, I liked your *Cluster of Bubbles* theory," remarked Derick.

"Yeah, well, I still like the bubble theory too, but I was thinking -- time could also have other forms. For instance, it could flow like a figure eight or infinity symbol, looping and crossing at the center," Calder continued.

"The place where time crosses could be where the portal lies," surmised Joe.

"Exactly! In the photography class, the image inverted when the light passed through a pinhole to the other side. Well, maybe those medieval kids are the inverted versions of us, living a parallel existence, only in a different space/time!" Calder continued excitedly. "There could even be multiple layers of time, like pages in a book. Just because you haven't read the last page yet, doesn't mean it doesn't exist! All moments might exist simultaneously, but on different planes or space/times, but we don't experience them until we arrive at that page. How do we know it's not so?"

"Wow, that's profound, Calder! I mean totally mind-boggling. Let's go have a double scoop of ice cream to cool you off," exclaimed Joe excitedly.

As they walked towards the ice cream stall they continued their conversation:

"When you think about it, people on the other side of the world from us don't feel as though they are upside down, even though their feet are facing towards our feet," postulated Azule. "So, wherever you are, your reality might feel -- correct."

"That's because we're blissfully unaware of any other existences. We're in our own separate *reality bubbles*. Space and gravity take care of the rest of the illusion," continued Calder, "but really, there could be all kinds of parallel universes." He paused to order his double scoop, "Rocky road and vanilla, please," then started right back where he left off. "Space is three-dimensional, time is the fourth dimension -- together they form the space/time continuum. Hmmm, energy cannot be destroyed, its form just morphs! So, maybe our energies morphed into medieval Calder, Hugo, Thomas, and Abigail!"

"Yeah, or vice versa," added Joe.

"I bet everybody has a *doppelganger* that they don't know about," mused Derick, preparing to order his double scoop on a waffle cone.

The double scoops certainly cooled off their hot conversation as they silently made their way over to the lunch benches. Azule looked at the stack of *Solar Flares*. What had started out as a pile of two hundred had now dwindled to only a handful. She was very happy to find that they had earned $64.75 towards their sixth-grade *Grad* party. Once again the magazines had been successful.

They'd had a plethora of essays and poems in this month's issue, the crossword puzzle had been won by a third-grader, and two more budding Picassos had been discovered. Azule's rhyming poem had received a lot of attention, although she didn't really feel that she deserved full credit for it. In her mind it was Abigail's, so she had printed it under her new pseudonym: Abigail of Camelot.

As the group of *time-navigators* sat on a lunch bench glancing through the book of English castles, pondering time, and overlooking the remnants of their school's version of May Day, Joe reached for one of the remaining *Solar Flares*.

"Read it to us, Azule," he coaxed nostalgically. "Read it and take us back to the manor and the moat."

"Should I?" asked Azule, feeling a little embarrassed, but seeing that the boys were waiting with anticipation. "Oh, alright!" she said, straightening her back and holding the magazine in front of her at page six:

Into the bog of eternal stench,
Rode a wench
On a horse-like bench.

Her heart was a-clench
For the men she let die
In a trench.
It was a dream
Pinned down by a scream,
For she did not mean
To be mean
To the men in her dream.

As the stream turned her green,
She awoke and spoke.
Alas, no-one was listening,
Nor saw the words glistening,

As they drowned in the babble
Of the stream.

And the dream went on,
And on, past the night,
But her eyes were glued tight,
So she saw not the light
When the day hit its height.

And she s t r e t c h e d
Over a day
And a thousand years,
Into the night of mares.

Fear not the goblins and ghouls,
Those are for fools,
Said the limpid pools
Of water, below where she lay.

Fear not death,
Nor the dragon's breath,
For they will be yours for a day.
Fear only yourself,
Young wench on the bench,
For you have the power of extremes
As told in your dreams.

Of day and of night,
Of play and of fight,
Of wrong and right,
And wealth and plight.

*But grasp both ends and hold on tight.
You may find the balance is just right.*

    Azule sat back and looked at the boys. For once they were all silent as though lost in a dream. She folded the magazine again and laid it on the pile.
    Azule had brought quite a few people together. No-one had been excluded thanks to her. Little *Miss Bookworm* had now become a popular magazine publisher -- and a poet.

Vanishing Point

Azule, Sarah, and Adam arrived at the same time and knocked on Jenna's front door. They were returning for the film-making summer camp after the sixth grade had drawn to a close. They felt older and wiser this year, and they certainly were taller and ready to move to junior high.

Jenna opened the door to greet them, "You've all grown so much! Come in." The art room looked much as it had the previous summer. The view through the panoramic windows showed the wall where Calder had performed for the photography lesson. It was now covered with trailing vines, shocking pink and purple geraniums, and numerous potted plants. In the corner of the room stood the tripod, this year crowned with a digital movie camera.

Azule pulled out a chair from the end of the long work table and Sarah sat to her right. In front of each student were sketchpads, placemats, and an assortment of moldable clay in a variety of colors. Adam chose a place halfway down the table and Calder pulled out the chair opposite him. The two friends hadn't seen each other for a few months; they'd both been extremely busy with camp, graduation, and other end-of-year activities.

"I can bring the fog machine again," offered Adam.

"Great, we can use it for special F.X.," Calder replied. Adam always had the coolest gadgets. Calder had missed getting together with him.

"How was your grad party?" asked Adam, but before Calder could answer, Adam proceeded to tell him about his own party. "We had a live band and Hawaiian dancers on the stage. Our parents rented a *limo* for ten of us. It was the BEST!"

Calder thought the limousine was over-indulgent, but he just laughed and admitted that his graduation was good, but not that great. "Ours was basically just a pizza party, the usual blahdy-blah speeches, and a pop song that I hope I'll never hear again!" he confessed. Still, they had both graduated from elementary school, and they both had fun celebrating the occasion. *Each to his own style* was Calder's new motto. They went on to talk about camp, and of course, according to Adam, his was the GREATEST camp ever!

Joe and Derick met at the street corner and walked down to Calder's house, arriving at the exact moment Jade and Ellie were being dropped off. Azule had spread the word about the summer class, so Jade and Ellie had decided that it would be fun to be part of the movie-making process too. Maddy couldn't make it, she was spending the summer with her cousins.

Jenna focused the students' attention on a very old carousel-type gadget with little, vertical slits all around the outer disc and slits and pictures on the inner disc.

"Would anyone like to guess what this is?" she began. Nobody had any idea. "It's a *phenakitiscope*," she explained, "and I didn't even know its name until recently. It's pronounced fenna-kitty-scope, and it's a motion viewer from the late nineteenth century, before movie cameras ever existed." She always gave a little history of the subject before class began. Jenna's great grandfather had been one of the early photographers in England. She had inherited a few of these *magic-lantern* contraptions from him. She brought them down from the attic for the film-making class.

"How does it work?" asked Joe, peering into the moving carousel.

"It's all about illusion," she began. "When you look through the slots, your eyes see a series of still pictures, each slightly different from the last." She set the inner disc spinning. "As it spins, the images appear to blend together, tricking your eye into perceiving the pictures as moving. Just like flip books, it gives the illusion of motion." Jenna showed an example. Flipping through the pages, her tiny stick man jumped in the air and turned head over heels. She then allowed a few minutes for the students to create their own flip books.

"Now let's try *claymation*," Jenna suggested. Some students were already busy, rolling out long multi-colored tube shapes. "We'll start out easy, spelling with snakes!" Jenna cleared the dining room table and placed a sheet of black card on top. The camera was secured to the tall tripod and a spotlight hung from a nearby cupboard handle, both aiming onto the table.

Joe wanted to be first to film his name for the

movie credits and his name was short enough to use as an example. Jenna positioned some clay letters on the board to spell out: **Animation by.** She filmed it to the count of three, then proceeded with Joe's name. He positioned his first clay snake at one corner and Jenna pressed the advance button. Joe moved the snake in tiny increments towards the center -- Jenna filmed. She waited until his hands were out of the frame after each movement, then filmed one short burst at a time. When sped up, the snake would appear to be slithering along fairly smoothly. Two tiny snakes arrived at a central position and formed the J. Joe had the next snake spin several turns before stopping to form the letter O. His last snake slithered along, curved around, and folded in on itself, forming the **e**.

"At sixteen frames per second the eye sees smooth movement," explained Jenna. "Has anyone seen a Charlie Chaplin silent movie?"

"Yeah, jerky-motion!" answered Derick.

"That's because they filmed less than sixteen frames per second in the early days of movie-making. More frames, less jerky," explained Jenna. "But of course, now it's all digitized, so we don't need to worry."

It took all afternoon to film their names, so Jenna had the rest of the group discuss the plans for their film. The consensus was for a medieval theme. Jenna suggested they all work together to figure out a storyline, then sketch their characters, and plan their costumes. They decided to create a multi-media film. For the main part, they would be using live actors mixed with a dose of cartoon animation, then the clay animation for their title and credits.

While they were sketching, Jenna inserted a DVD and they watched "Wallace and Grommit", a series of *claymation* films by Nick Parks. After that, she showed them a film from 1902 by George Melies entitled *Le Voyage dans la Lune*, or *A Trip to the Moon*. A rocket hits the moon-face smack in the eye. Jenna told them that this movie had been quite innovative in the history of special effects.

At first the students had conflicting ideas about how their story should unfold, but Jenna encouraged them to write everything down.

"Out of chaos comes order," she reassured. "We just have to unravel it as we go along, but remember, we only have five days to pull this all together!"

"We could have a mutant iguana attacking some dinosaurs," suggested Adam.

"It's a medieval film! Advance a few million years, Adam!" quipped Calder impatiently. They frowned at each other, then cracked up laughing.

"Azule should definitely be our Guinevere," proposed Derick, remembering Abigail at Kirkfield. Joe and Calder agreed wholeheartedly. Azule just smiled.

"Who is Guinevere?" asked Sarah. "And can I be Juliet?"

"Haven't you ever heard of King Arthur and the Knights of the Round Table?" asked Joe.

"Well yes I think so -- Camelot, right?" guessed Sarah correctly.

"Well, Guinevere was King Arthur's wife, but she and Lancelot had a secret love," explained Joe. Azule just blushed.

"There'll be no smoochy stuff in our movie," bellowed Calder. "Just *Pomp and Circumstance!*"

Jade suggested a medieval May Day carnival.

"Yeah, sort of a Renaissance Faire," added Derick.

"We could have a turnip shy and market stalls selling hot cross buns," suggested Joe.

"We have stilts, and whiffle balls to juggle, and musical instruments to play." offered Calder. "I wanna be the jester!"

"I can bring my T-rex costume -- and I have MORE musical instruments," echoed Adam.

The plans for the first scene were now falling into place. Sarah and Jade offered to make the tall pointed cone hats with chiffon flowing from the peaks, which were often associated with the Middle Ages. Jenna supplied them with sheets of pastel colored card and showed them how to curl them into cone-shaped hats. All they had to do then was cut off the excess card, glue and staple the seams, and attach the delicate chiffon scarves.

As Monday's class came to a close, Jenna sat down with the group at the long table in the back room. She scribbled down some notes and created a punch list of props and fabrics to find.

"Should we bring our costumes tomorrow?" asked Sarah excitedly.

"Yes! If you have costumes or props, bring them in," answered Jenna.

"Should I bring the fog machine?" asked Adam.

"Yeah, that would be so cool for the moat scene," answered Joe leaning back on his chair.

"What moat scene?" asked Jade.

"Well, a few of us already have an idea -- half thought out," Azule hesitated. "Joe, Derick, Calder, and I often talk about medieval times."

Sarah shot Ellie a disbelieving glance. They were

beginning to feel that Azule and the boys had an agenda all of their own.

"It's just a vague theme, but you can add your own ideas to it," suggested Azule, sensing Sarah's contention and not wanting to discourage anyone's creative input.

"It's set in the late 1400's in a medieval village in England..." began Joe.

"The ancient market place is bustling with medieval merchants and villagers..." continued Derick.

"In the valley a manor house stands, surrounded by a deep, dark, watery moat..." added Calder, the way he had begun his tale at camp.

"Oh, yeah, I remember! I liked that story, Calder," admitted Ellie.

"Can't we have a mutant iguana battling a fiery dragon?" pleaded Adam.

"Actually, there was a dragon!" Azule, Calder, Derick, and Joe yelled in unison, then followed up with -- "JINX!"

"Could I be Juliet?" pleaded Sarah once again.

"Well, we could incorporate a Juliet-type character into our movie, but you should make up your own story about her," suggested Joe.

Jenna sensed the tension and tried to refocus them by letting each one propose a character and a situation. She began with Ellie, and the atmosphere immediately softened.

The students were diligent in their search for costumes. With the help of enthusiastic parents, a fully dressed cast of characters showed up at Jenna's house the following morning.

"Fantastic!" she exclaimed upon opening the door. Jenna

enjoyed their commitment and enthusiasm. "We're almost halfway there," she beamed.

Costumes were tried and altered, headwear successfully constructed, fabric folded and stitched to make simple tunics and cloaks for the boys, and their swords were ceremoniously stashed into their long hipster belts.

Jenna produced a long, thick wooden curtain rod, to be used as a lance for the mock-jousting tournament. Derick helped her saw the end off a plastic oil funnel and he slid it onto the pole to create the vamplate, or hand-guard. It was now looking more and more like a jousting lance.

"We must pad the end. We want no accidents," cautioned Jenna, searching for a wad of bubble wrap and a roll of duct tape.

"We can use these two saw horses as the knights' chargers," suggested Joe.

"Of course, the wench on a horse-like bench!" declared Azule, referring to Abigail's poem, which was now strangely beginning to make sense. Azule sat side-saddle on one of the saw horses, both legs to one side emulating the lady in the poem. She had perfectly straight posture and her hands were poised as though she was holding the reins of a proud Lipizzaner stallion.

Calder returned wearing his Norman helmet, his pajama bottoms for leggings, and a long-sleeved thermal shirt with a green corduroy tunic over the top (a length of fabric with a hole cut out for the head). His leather pouch and his sword were attached to a long leather belt, tied at his hips. Around his shoulders Calder wore the red cloak, which Jenna had made from the velvet curtain he had photographed a year earlier. Once again his demeanor was serious.

"Wow, Calder you look great!" was all that Azule could say.

"Hmmm, yeah, Sir Prance-a-lot!" quipped Sarah.

"You look like the knight in your drawing," added Ellie.

"I *am*," retorted Calder proudly. "I'm Calder, the Millennium Knight."

After a lunch break, Derick and Calder collaborated on creating title boards in order to set the scene for each act:

<u>Scene One</u>: "The Market Place" -- wrote Derick. Calder illustrated it with a sketch of the ancient Thornhill cross, a few market stalls, and a maypole.

<u>Scene Two</u>: "The Manor and the Moat" --

"And Four Fair Maidens!" suggested Joe.

<u>Scene Three</u>: "Knights of the L-o-n-g Table" -- Calder giggled mischievously, and quickly drew stick men wearing helmets seated along a very extensive table.

<u>Scene Four</u>: "The Slaying of Draconis" -- oodles of red painted dragon blood here.

<u>Scene Five</u>: "The Jousting Tournament" -- crossed lances and more red paint!

<u>Scene Six</u>: "Much Merriment in Camelot" -- Calder sketched Guinevere and Arthur in the stone castle archway.

<u>Scene Seven</u>: "Lancelot Rides Off Alone into the Mists of Avalon" -- Calder drew the back of a shire horse with his armored knight sitting astride it, and mist rising from the forest floor. He spent more time on this sketch, as he liked the subject matter.

By Wednesday, several drapes and flags graced the

high deck and edged the walls, emulating the fair City of York. The patio became the market square with a turnip shy and a few stalls. With Calder's help, Jenna had attached reams of multi-colored paper streamers to the top corner post of the patio to serve as their maypole.

On the other side of the art room, the honeysuckle garden with the old stone bird bath became the entrance to the manor for scene two. Jenna had once again recycled some black plastic sheeting as the deep, dark moat. Azule sprinkled clover and sour grass upon it to create a carpet of lime-green duckweed, and Adam's fog machine was on hand to create the mysterious, misty atmosphere.

Order was finally emerging from the chaos, and the kids were so busy with their epic production that the days had flown by. Adam had brought his rubber Tyrannosaurus Rex costume and it actually made a perfect dragon! His persistence had paid off. Jenna filmed a close-up shot of their pet iguana, then blended into a shot of the T-Rex foot ferociously clawing the air. Joe pumped intermittent blasts of fog from behind the T-Rex's mouth and it certainly created the illusion of a dragon's fiery breath.

"Okay, it's a wrap!" Jenna called with authority. Adam roared loudly as he pulled off the suffocating rubber mask. Jade, who was standing next to him, screamed with terror and the other girls giggled.

For lunch there were some delicious, traditional English treats, which had been provided by most of the moms to help Jenna with the baking task.

"We'll save a few for the market stall tomorrow, but we have plenty, so tuck in!" offered Jenna.

During the break, Azule and the three boys wandered around to the honeysuckle garden, to discuss the possibility of opening another time portal and inverting through to their counterparts at the moat. Ever since their last journey they had wanted to return to experience the lives of Calder, Hugo, Thomas, and Abigail -- just once more!

Calder suggested they try to create the infinity symbol by dancing a Scottish reel. They practiced first linking right arms, then left arms with the next partner. Pretty soon they had it flowing smoothly, in a never-ending figure eight. "We'll be ready to go by tomorrow," said Calder confidently.

The students fizzed with excitement when Thursday rolled around. They had rehearsed the play several times, and now wearing full costume, they were ready to become not only movie stars, but also producers, animators, directors, and by Friday, editors too. The premier would then be presented to an audience of eager parents.

The completed storyboards were displayed against the fence and filming was about to begin. Each girl had found a long dress that needed the medieval touch. Jenna added crossed ribbons at the waists and accessorized with cloaks and posies of pickle-weed and clover. The headdresses, with their floating chiffon veils completed the look of the medieval maidens.

Calder juggled three hacky-sack balls poorly, most of them landing on his helmet. Adam balanced precariously on wooden stilts, preparing for his grand entrance, and Derick showed off his impressive yo-yo skills. Joe was busy throwing a wooden ball at the turnip shy, as the girls rehearsed their hand-clapping May Day song. A medieval hive of activity was in play.

"Get ready for the first scene," called Jenna. "Cameras ready to roll!"

She focused on the first storyboard, Scene One: "A Medieval Marketplace" as she counted off three seconds. Then switching to a long shot, and panning from left to right, she captured the medieval atmosphere as the renaissance activities unfolded. Next she focused on the four maidens, each at the end of a cascading ribbon, wending and weaving their way at the base of their maypole, singing:

"Hot cross buns, hot cross buns.
One a penny, two a penny,
Hot cross buns!"

Jenna zoomed in and lingered a few more moments on each individual character, before shouting:

"Cut!"

"Prepare to switch to scene two!"

Jenna then passed the camera to Adam, encouraging him to take over the movie production.

"No problem," he answered confidently. Taking charge, he zoomed in on the second storyboard, Scene Two: "The Manor and the Moat." Then on cue, the cast abandoned the marketplace to parade around the backyard, past the high deck to the honeysuckle garden on the other side of the art room. Adam was ahead of them, walking backwards to capture the advancing procession. A derisive mockingbird caught his attention as it squawked noisily at the flamboyant scene, flashing a warning with his gray and white plumage to the troupe below. Adam continued filming in case it could be edited into the story. Jenna had planned for each student to take a turn shooting a scene of the film. After all, this was their production.

Meanwhile, Calder, Joe, Derick, and Azule had moved ahead and were joyfully dancing their Scottish reel in order to open the new time portal. To all others, it looked as though they were rehearsing the moat scene in front of the birdbath. As the rest of the troupe arrived in the honeysuckle garden, the four *Time Navigators* positioned themselves at the entrance to the would-be manor hall, next to Magog (a.k.a. the stone birdbath).

Adam passed the camera to Sarah for her turn to film, then he went to switch on the fog machine. Ellie began to strum the guitar and Jade prepared to sing *Green Sleeves*, a ballad she'd been rehearsing all week. All cogs were now in motion.

Calder, Joe, Derick, and Azule looked into each other's eyes. For a split second, each one knew what the others were thinking: This was their opportunity to visit their counterparts in the Middle Ages. The four friends focused their gaze on the slick black recycled plastic, which symbolized the deep, dark waters of the moat at Thornhill Hall. Had they been successful in opening a new time portal to the past? Carpe Diem! They were excited and ready to seize the day!

As the fog machine's ethereal mist rose in hovering wisps around their ankles, Jenna raised her hand and shouted:

"Lights -- Camera -- Action!!"